Into the Dark . . .

He put his arm around her shoulders, guiding her away from the cliff and back toward the woods behind the road. "We'll walk this way," he said softly. "I like the woods at night, don't you?"

"It's a little cold," Chelsea said with a shiver, her breath steaming in front of her, white against the black night. "But I like it," she added quickly. "It's so peaceful up here."

He slowed his pace, let Chelsea get a few steps ahead. Then he pulled the length of cord from his jacket pocket, silently untangled it, and pulled it taut between his hands with a silent snap.

Don't miss these chilling tales from

FEAR STREET®

All-Night Party

The Confession

First Date

Killer's Kiss

The Perfect Date

The Rich Girl

Secret Admirer

The Stepsister

After hours, the horror continues at

FEAR STREET® NIGHTS

#1: Moonlight Secrets

#2: Midnight Games

#3: Darkest Dawn

R.L. STINE

FEAR STREET®

FIRST DATE

Simon Pulse
New York London Toronto Sydney

A Parachute Press book

SIMON PULSE
An imprint of Simon & Schuster Children's Publishing Division
1230 Avenue of the Americas, New York, NY 10020
Copyright © 1992 by Parachute Publishing, L.L.C.
All rights reserved, including the right of reproduction in whole or in part in any form.
SIMON PULSE and colophon are registered trademarks of
Simon & Schuster, Inc.
FEAR STREET is a registered trademark of Parachute Press, Inc.
Designed by Sammy Yuen Jr.
The text of this book was set in Times.
Manufactured in the United States of America
First Simon Pulse edition January 2006
10 9 8 7 6 5
Library of Congress Control Number 2005921099
ISBN-13: 978-1-4169-0819-7
ISBN-10: 1-4169-0819-6

FIRST DATE

chapter

1

"We can't see out, and no one can see in," she said, snuggling against his shoulder. "It's like we're in our own private world."

He smiled at her and hugged her closer. He kissed her, a long, lingering kiss. She closed her eyes. He kept his wide open, staring at the windshield, which was completely steamed over as if covered by a white blanket.

It's so hot in this car, he thought, kissing her again.

I can't breathe.

I've got to get some air. Or I'll die.

She pulled her head back and smiled up at him dreamily. "Joe," she whispered.

He stared at the windshield, imagining the night beyond it, picturing the tall, wet grass, the dark trees.

Can't breathe. Can't breathe.

She pressed her forehead against his chest and sighed. He could smell oranges in her hair. He could still taste her lipstick on his mouth, sweet and sour at the same time.

What was her name, anyway?

Holding her close, he tried to remember.

Candy.

That was it. Candy Something-or-Other.

It's so steamy in here.

I feel so . . . locked in. Trapped. As if the car is closing in on me.

"I've never been up here with a boy before," she said, pressing her face against his leather jacket.

She's smothering me, he thought. I'm going to smother in here.

Why does it have to be so steamy?

He slid his arm away from her and reached for the window handle. He started to roll down his window, but she grabbed his arm. "No. Don't. Someone might see."

"But we're all alone up here," he said. "We're lucky there are no other cars tonight." He took a long, deep breath of cool air before closing the window. Outside, he caught a glimpse of the moon, a pale gray sliver low in the sky.

"I like you, Joe," Candy said as he moved his arm back around her shoulder.

"I like you too," he said automatically, immedi-

2

ately wishing he had sounded more sincere. He kissed her ear.

I'm sweating, he thought. It's October and I'm sweating.

I'm going to suffocate.

She's going to suffocate me.

"I like boys with curly black hair," she whispered. She brushed her hand tenderly through his hair.

I hate that, he realized.

Mom used to do that to me.

"Let's go for a walk," he suggested, reaching for the door handle.

"I don't know. Is it safe?" Her dark eyes gleamed with excitement.

He shrugged. "I don't come up here much, either."

Rainer's Point was the big make-out spot for Central High kids. The narrow road stopped at a grassy clearing that sloped to the edge of a steep rock cliff. Behind the clearing were thick woods.

It was silent out there, except for a whisper of wind through the trees.

"Come on," he urged, squeezing her hand. "I'll protect you."

She giggled for some reason.

He pushed open the car door, bathing them in harsh yellow light.

"Wait, Joe," she said and reached down to the car floor. "You dropped your wallet."

"Oh. Thanks." He reached for it.

But he saw it come open. Then he saw her eyes grow wide as she stared at his driver's license inside.

"Joe—?" She raised her eyes to him, questioning him.

Here we go, he thought, his heart racing.

"Joe Hodge," she said, returning her glance to the driver's license. "You told me your name was Joe Hodge. But your license says Lonnie Mayes."

"It's—someone else's license," he said.

I can't breathe.

I'm suffocating.

The car door is open, and I'm still suffocating.

Don't suffocate me, Candy. I'm warning you. Don't do it.

She tossed her long brown hair. It fell quickly back into place. Her expression was thoughtful, troubled. "But it's your picture on the license," she said. She held it up to show him, as if he hadn't seen it before.

He sighed.

What a shame, he thought.

Why does she want to suffocate me?

Why is she accusing me?

"I lost my license," he said, taking the wallet

4

from her hand. "So I'm using this one." He pushed the wallet into his jacket pocket.

"So you're Joe Hodge? You're not Lonnie Mayes?" she asked, wrinkling her forehead.

What a shame, he thought.

Shame, shame, shame.

He pushed the car door open the rest of the way and slid out. He stood up, arched his back, his hands in his jacket pockets, and stretched. Then he took a deep breath, leaned back in, and smiled reassuringly at her.

"Come on, Candy. Let's take a walk. A short one. It's so nice out here. And there's no one here tonight. No one around for miles."

No one, he thought, his mind whirring, his muscles tensing.

No one around for miles.

He suddenly felt very alert. Ready.

She stepped out of the car and closed the door. The car light went out, leaving them in darkness.

Taking long, deliberate steps, he crossed the clearing, dew from the tall grass clinging to his shoes, and stared down over the cliff edge. There was nothing but darkness below.

She stepped up beside him and reached for his hand. Her hand felt hot and wet in his. She lowered her eyes to the cliff edge.

"Can we back up?" she asked in a pleading whisper. "I have a problem with heights."

5

"Sure," he said. He began leading her across the clearing toward the trees, walking slowly, squeezing her hand tightly.

What a shame. What a shame.

"How old are you?" she asked suddenly.

I'm twenty, he thought.

"Seventeen," he said.

"How did you lose your driver's license so soon? Were you in an accident or something?"

You're the one who's going to have an accident, he thought.

A fatal accident.

If only you hadn't tried to suffocate me.

If only your hair wasn't the same dark color as—hers.

"No. I just lost it," he said softly.

He put his arm around her shoulder and drew her close as he led her under the trees. "I like you, Candy," he said, whispering into her ear.

Again, he smelled oranges in her hair.

Did he really like her?

Was he lying to her?

He couldn't be sure. He didn't know.

He only knew it was a shame she had to die.

A real shame.

A few minutes later he walked slowly, calmly back to the car. Alone. His heart was racing in his chest, but otherwise, he felt fine.

Just fine. Killing her was so easy.

He zipped his leather jacket, then climbed behind the wheel. The car started quickly. He started the defroster and sat waiting for the windshield to clear.

The air from the defroster felt dry and cold.

He laughed out loud, a giddy laugh, a laugh of release.

The fog on the windshield began to clear.

"Joe Hodge," he said aloud. I told her my name was Joe Hodge.

Why should I tell her my real name? It was our first date, after all.

Our first date.

He hadn't planned on murdering her tonight.

He liked her. He really liked her.

She didn't remind him so much of the others. Just her hair. The long brown hair.

He wasn't really prepared for this one.

Why did she have to suffocate him? Why did she have to toss her hair like that? Why did she have to see the driver's license?

Why did she have to ask so many questions?

Why didn't she let him *breathe?*

He wasn't prepared. He hadn't planned it.

He always liked to plan it.

But she was dead anyway.

I'll be out of here by the time they find her, he thought.

I haven't left any traces. No one was here.

7

I'll be okay.

Now at least I can breathe again.

The windshield was clear. He turned on the headlights and started to back up onto the road.

On to another town.

Sooner or later it was time to move on.

He didn't really like it that way, but what choice did he have?

What choice did he have if girls looked like that? If they asked him questions and wouldn't let him breathe?

He pushed the gearshift into Park, then reached into the glove compartment.

His hand wasn't shaking.

That was a good sign.

He could breathe again, and his hand wasn't shaking.

He turned on the light, pulled out the road map, unfolded it carefully, his hands steady. His eyes darted over the map and stopped at the name of the next town.

Shadyside.

He mouthed the word several times, silently to himself.

Shadyside.

Sounds like my kind of place.

He replaced the worn, wrinkled map, switched off the ceiling light, then, humming softly to himself, roared off into the cool, silent darkness.

chapter
2

Chelsea Richards blew a sour *honk* and pulled the saxophone from her mouth in disgust. "I hate my life," she said flatly and without emotion.

"Don't start," her mother said quietly from across the small living room. She lowered the newspaper enough to give Chelsea a warning look, a look that said "I'm not in the mood to hear your usual list of complaints."

Chelsea fingered the saxophone, leaning over in the folding chair she used for practice, nearly bumping her head on the music stand in front of her. "Sometimes I think I'm not a real member of this family," she complained, ignoring her mother's warning glance. "I mean, like I'm adopted or something."

"You weren't adopted. You were hatched," Mrs. Richards cracked, hidden behind her newspaper. "Are you through practicing that thing—I hope?"

"You hate my saxophone playing," Chelsea accused.

"You were playing it? I thought you were *torturing* it!" Mrs. Richards said and laughed.

Chelsea was used to her mother's dry sense of humor. Sometimes it helped snap Chelsea out of a bad mood, but not now. "You really crack yourself up, don't you?" Chelsea said angrily.

I don't have my mother's good looks, and I don't even have her sense of humor, she thought bitterly.

"If I'm not adopted, how come you're so tall and thin and I'm so short and dumpy?" Chelsea asked, pulling off the mouthpiece and blowing the saliva out of it.

"Chelsea, please!" her mother cried impatiently. She lowered the newspaper to her lap and shook her head. "Why do you like to have the same conversations over and over?"

"At least it's a conversation," Chelsea replied with growing anger. "Usually we just grunt at each other before you hurry off to work."

"Boy, you have a million complaints today— don't you," her mother said. "I'm very sorry, but your father and I have to work very hard. It's not like you're bringing in a fortune with your saxophone playing."

"Hey, I work in Dad's restaurant. I earn my own money," Chelsea snapped. "Stop giving me a hard time about my music. It's the only thing I enjoy."

The *only* thing, Chelsea repeated to herself.

The only thing in my whole miserable life.

"Why are you feeling so sorry for yourself these days?" Mrs. Richards asked. She put the newspaper down on the coffee table and walked over to Chelsea.

Chelsea shrugged. "It's this new town. Shady-side. And this creepy old house."

"Please stop complaining about the house. We'll fix it up," Mrs. Richards said, crossing her slender arms over her pale blue turtleneck. "You know your father has always dreamed of owning his own restaurant, Chelsea. Moving here is a great opportunity for him. For all of us."

"The kids at school tell stories about this street. Fear Street. They say all kinds of weird things happen here."

"Weird things happen everywhere," her mother said dryly. She glanced at the window. The clouds were drifting apart. Afternoon sunlight filtered into the room.

Chelsea finished taking apart her instrument. She placed the sections carefully into their slots, then closed the case.

"Why don't I have straight hair like yours?" Chelsea demanded, realizing she should quit but unable to do it. "Why does my hair have to be so curly and this awful mousy brown color?"

"You want to change your hair color?" her mother asked, surprised. "That's easy to do."

"Then how do I change my face?" Chelsea cried, glancing into the mirror on the wall by the entryway.

My nose is too wide and my chin is too small, she thought for the millionth time.

"Chelsea, you're a very attractive girl," her mother said, her arms still crossed. "If you'd lose a little weight and put on some lipstick—"

Chelsea uttered a cry of disgust and jumped up from the chair. Her mother, startled, took a step back.

"Mom, give me a break. Don't say I'm *attractive.* That's what you say about people who aren't. Why don't you just say I have a *nice* personality and be done with it? That's what people always say about ugly girls. They have nice personalities."

"Frankly, your looks are great. It's your personality I'm not crazy about," her mother said, doing her impression of a stand-up comic.

"Mom—" Chelsea screamed, feeling herself lose control. "Can't you *ever* be serious?"

Mrs. Richards stepped forward and wrapped her daughter in an awkward hug. The gesture caught Chelsea by surprise. Her mother was not given to outward displays of affection. Chelsea couldn't remember the last time her mother had hugged her.

"I-I'm sorry, Mom," she blurted out, not exactly sure why she was apologizing.

"Ssshhh." Mrs. Richards raised a finger to Chelsea's lips. Then she took a step back. "It's having to move here, dear," she said, staring reassuringly into Chelsea's eyes. "It's having to start all over again in a new town, at a new high school. That's what's making you so—edgy."

Chelsea nodded, thinking about what her mother was saying.

"And you're unhappy because your dad is always at the restaurant and I'm always at the nursing home taking care of patients instead of being home with you. But we can't help it, Chelsea. This is a great opportunity for us. Especially for your father. If he can make this restaurant work, he'll be so happy. And we can get out of debt."

Mrs. Richards shoved her hands into the pockets of her jeans and began to pace back and forth across the small room. "Don't get down on yourself. That's all I ask," she told Chelsea. "You can be down on your situation, on having to move. But don't start doubting yourself."

Chelsea glanced in the mirror again. Easy for her to say, she thought unhappily. She's tall and pretty. And I look like a cow.

"Okay, Mom," she said with false brightness. "You're right. I'm sorry."

Her mother's face revealed her worry. "You've made one good friend here already, haven't you?"

Chelsea nodded. "Nina Darwin."

"Why don't you give her a call?" Mrs. Richards suggested. "She seems really nice. And really popular. I'm sure she'll introduce you to a lot of other kids."

She glanced at her watch. "Oh, wow. I'm late. Got to run." She gave Chelsea a quick, dry kiss on the forehead and, after gathering up her keys and wallet from the hallway table, hurried out the door.

Chelsea sighed.

What was *that* all about? she asked herself. Mom's right. I've got to stop feeling sorry for myself.

She carried her saxophone into her room and slid it into the closet. Then she pulled off her white sweatshirt, which suddenly felt hot and uncomfortable, and searched for something cooler to put on.

I've got to get out of this house, she thought, yanking a lime green T-shirt out of her drawer. Maybe Nina can cheer me up.

Nina Darwin lived a few blocks away, only a ten-minute walk from Chelsea's house. Chelsea had met Nina in the Shadyside High marching band.

They had met by accident.

A real accident.

Nina played flute, and the two of them had marched right into each other during the band's first after-school practice. Chelsea's saxophone had received a slight dent, and Nina's knee was slightly scraped. Other than that, they were both uninjured.

They had become good friends after that, although at practice Nina always insisted on marching on the other side of the field from Chelsea.

Nina was short and perky looking, with sharp, small features and straight, white blond hair. Unlike Chelsea, she had a relaxed, easygoing personality and seemed to have a million friends.

She looks about twelve, Chelsea sometimes thought. When we walk together, people probably think I'm her mother!

"Don't get down on yourself," Chelsea said out loud, repeating her mother's advice.

Nina was a good friend. The only friend she'd made at Shadyside High so far.

So don't start finding fault with her, Chelsea warned herself.

Chelsea felt herself cheering up a little as she walked to Nina's house. It was a clear autumn day, the air tangy and dry. Leaves on the trees were just starting to turn. Some of the houses on Fear Street were old and run-down, but they didn't seem frightening or evil, the way she'd heard kids describe them.

As she crossed onto Nina's street, a car drove by,

windows down, its radio blaring. Chelsea recognized some kids from school inside. They were laughing and singing and didn't seem to notice her as they roared past.

Nina's house—a long, redwood, ranch-style house—stood at the top of a steeply sloping lawn. Even though it was autumn the grass had recently been cut.

Just as Chelsea stepped up to the front door, it opened. Nina appeared, followed by her boyfriend, Doug Fredericks, a lanky, handsome boy with long blond hair and a friendly, winning grin.

Nina's mouth dropped open in surprise. "Chelsea! Where'd you come from?"

"Home," Chelsea replied, pointing in the general direction of her house.

"Hi," Doug said, moving Nina out of the way so he could close the glass storm door.

"I didn't know—" Nina started.

"I should've called," Chelsea said quickly.

"We're just going to Doug's cousin's," Nina said. "Why don't you come?"

"Yeah. Come on," Doug said, motioning for Chelsea to follow him as he headed for his car, a shiny red Toyota. "We're just going to talk and stuff."

"No, I don't think so," Chelsea said. "Thanks. I'll call you later."

"Okay." Nina shrugged. "You're welcome to come."

Go with them, urged a tiny voice in Chelsea's mind.

But then another tiny voice said, Three's a crowd.

"No. Go ahead," Chelsea said.

Doug was already in the car. He blew the horn. Nina went running down the walk. A few seconds later Chelsea watched them drive away.

Walking home, she felt sorry for herself all over again.

Doug blows the horn and Nina comes running, she thought bitterly.

I'd come running too, if I had a boyfriend.

A boyfriend? I'd just like to go out on a date, she thought.

Here I am fifteen, and I haven't gone out on my first date yet.

Just as she thought that, Chelsea heard a car pull up behind her. Startled, she stopped walking as a boy called out, "Hey, how about a date?"

chapter

3

Chelsea spun around to see four grinning boys in a tiny Honda Civic. The kid in the front passenger seat had stringy brown hair tied back in a ponytail and a diamond stud in one ear. He stuck a hand out of the open window as if reaching for her. "How about it?"

Chelsea made a face and started to walk away, taking long, fast strides.

The car inched forward slowly, keeping right at her heels.

"How about it?" the kid repeated. "How about a date?"

"Plenty of room in here," another voice said.

The car rang with high-pitched laughter.

Chelsea kept walking, picking up the pace. The car inched forward, staying right beside her.

She heard more laughter. One of the boys made loud kissing noises.

"Come on. We're nice guys," the kid with the ponytail said, grinning at her, his hand still out the window.

"We're great. We're really great," a boy called from the backseat.

"Bet you're great too," another voice from the backseat echoed.

More laughter.

Chelsea spun around angrily. "Leave me alone," she snapped, glaring at the four boys.

"Aw, that's not friendly," one of them said.

"Don't you want to be friendly?" another called out.

They all laughed.

"I'm warning you—" Chelsea started.

"Ooh, she's getting steamed," the driver said.

"That's not friendly," another boy said.

Chelsea realized her heart was thudding in her chest. Her anger was giving way to fear.

Were they just teasing her? Were they eventually going to drive away? Or did they really plan to harm her?

She stared into the car, studying each grinning face. She didn't recognize any of them. They didn't go to Shadyside, she was fairly certain.

"Come on, let's all get friendly," the passenger pleaded, reaching out for her. The driver pulled the car up beside her so the stringy-haired kid could grab for her arm.

"No!" Chelsea cried, leaping out of his grasp.

The four boys laughed.

"Leave me alone! I mean it!" Chelsea cried.

One of them flicked a lighted cigarette at her. It landed on top of one of her sneakers. She kicked it off and started to run.

Their laughter was loud and cruel.

Animals, she thought. They're just animals.

She was running up on the grass now, running up close to shrubs and low hedges. Breathing hard and gasping out loud as she ran, Chelsea listened for the car, listened for the laughter, the voices, listened for the sound of a door opening, the sound of one of them running after her.

When the tiny car roared past, its horn blaring, she stopped to catch her breath, her fear lingering, her legs trembling, her heart still pounding.

They're gone, she thought, watching the car squeal around the corner. She felt relieved and miserable.

If only something *good* would happen to me, she thought.

If only I could meet a guy who liked me.

The new boy at Shadyside High got the seat in homeroom next to Chelsea. It was the only vacant seat in the room, in the back row next to the wastebasket.

Chelsea studied him as he made his way down the long row toward her. He walked quickly, carrying his backpack in front of him, avoiding everyone's eyes. He was still wearing his leather jacket. Probably hasn't been assigned a locker yet, Chelsea decided.

He was average in height and weight and had dark eyes and black curly hair. He flashed Chelsea a shy smile as he took his seat, and she saw that he had powerful-looking, muscular arms that seemed too developed for the rest of him.

He caught her staring at him, and she quickly turned her head to the front, embarrassed.

Will Blakely.

That's what Mr. Carter had said his name was.

Will Blakely.

He's kind of cute, Chelsea thought, stealing another long glance at him. His dark eyes were lowered to the floor. His cheeks were bright pink.

He really is shy, Chelsea decided.

She wanted to say hi or welcome or something. But she couldn't.

I'm shy too, she thought. I *hate* being shy!

Mr. Carter was racing through the morning announcements, reading faster than the human ear could hear as usual. When he put the announcement sheet down for a minute, he surveyed the room, searching for empty seats.

"All present and accounted for," he said, marking something on his attendance sheet, his eyeglasses sliding down to the end of his long nose. "I think there's going to be a fire drill today. Hope you guys can take all the excitement."

Mr. Carter had a very dry sense of humor. But everyone always laughed and talked in homeroom so it was hard to hear a word he said!

The first-period bell rang. Chelsea glanced at Will, but he avoided her eyes. He ran a hand nervously through his black hair before starting to pull his backpack up from under his seat.

Chelsea stood up and started to hoist her backpack to her shoulder. "Oh, no!" she cried. Her notebooks, books, and supplies tumbled to the floor. She had forgotten to zip the bag.

She looked down to see her brown-paper lunchbag open, her sandwich at her feet, an apple rolling across the room.

With a loud sigh she stooped and began to collect her things. To her surprise, Will let go of his pack and dropped down beside her to help.

"Pretty stupid, huh?" she managed to say.

He smiled. His cheeks turned pinker. He stuffed the sandwich back in the bag and handed it to her.

Their eyes met for only a second. He quickly turned away.

He's even shyer than I am, she thought.

She found herself staring at his powerful biceps and quickly lowered her eyes to the floor.

Say something. Say *something!* she scolded herself.

"Thanks for helping," she said.

Brilliant! What a brilliant remark!

He shrugged and flashed her an awkward smile. Then he picked up his bag and walked quickly to the door without glancing back.

I *hate* being shy, Chelsea thought, still scolding herself.

But what can I do?

Another girl would have thought of something clever to say, something funny. Nina would have had him laughing his head off. Nina would have had him asking her out before her stuff was back in the backpack.

Why can't I be more like her?

I'll talk to him tomorrow morning, she decided, hurrying out into the crowded, noisy hallway.

I have a whole day to figure out what to say.

Having made this decision, Chelsea felt better. She was even smiling as she walked into her first-period English class and headed to her seat in the back row.

That evening Chelsea was thinking about Will while she worked in her father's restaurant. The

All-Star Café was a cramped, too brightly lit coffee shop on one of the narrow, run-down streets of the Old Village. That night Chelsea was the only waitress. There was really only room for one. Ernie, the fry cook, had called in sick. So her father, tired and disheartened, was behind the grill in the kitchen.

There were very few customers. Two old men drinking coffee at the end of the counter. A teenage boy and girl having club sandwiches and Cokes in the next-to-last booth near the back.

Chelsea found herself daydreaming about Will. She had decided what she was going to say to him. She was going to ask him if he worked out. Then she'd ask when his family had moved to Shadyside and where he lived.

A third old man entered and joined the two at the counter, calling to Chelsea for a cup of coffee. She picked up a cup, carried it to the coffeepot, poured it, and started to take it to the old man, all the while daydreaming about the conversation she and Will would have, imagining both roles.

"Oh, no!"

The heavy china cup slipped out of her hand and landed on the counter before crashing to the floor in front of it. It shattered into several pieces, coffee splattering everywhere.

Chelsea saw her father glaring at her from the kitchen. "I'll clean it up," she called to him.

Chelsea brought the old man another cup of

24

coffee. Then she picked up the broom and dustpan and bent over the broken china on the floor.

She picked up several large shards carefully by hand and dropped them into the dustpan. Then she climbed to her feet—and bumped into someone who had just entered.

"Oh! Sorry!" she cried, startled.

He grinned at her. "I enjoyed it," he cracked.

He looked about seventeen or eighteen. He had laughing dark eyes, a handsome, high-cheekboned face, and thick black hair.

He looks tough, Chelsea thought, staring at his black leather jacket with silver pocket zippers, his faded jeans torn at both knees. The jacket was partly unzipped, revealing a black and red Rolling Stones T-shirt underneath.

"Sorry. I'm in your way," Chelsea said, retreating behind the counter. She watched him walk to the far end of the counter. He seemed to swagger as he walked, as if daring someone to get in his way. When he wasn't flashing a crinkly-eyed smile, his expression was hard, tough.

Chelsea deposited the broken china into the wastebasket, then hurried to bring the boy a menu. He held up his hand, shaking the menu away. "I know what I want. Just a hamburger and a Coke."

"How would you like your hamburger?" Chelsea asked, wiping her hands on the long white apron her dad made her wear.

"Cooked," he said.

Chelsea could feel her face growing hot. She suddenly felt embarrassed. I must look like such a geek in this stupid apron with my hair pulled back, standing here asking him how he wants his hamburger.

"That was a joke," he said, his expression not changing.

Chelsea forced an awkward laugh. "I know," she said. She turned and called the order through the window to her father. He nodded, and she could hear the splat and sizzle of a hamburger hitting the grill.

"So what do you do for a living?" the boy asked, his dark eyes gleaming.

Chelsea stared at him, unable to think of a reply.

"That was another joke," he said. "Guess you're not in a joking mood, huh?"

"I don't hear too many jokes in here," Chelsea replied, picking up a rag and wiping the Formica counter.

"What's your name?" He was staring hard into her eyes as if challenging her to speak to him.

"Chelsea. Chelsea Richards." She realized he was the first customer ever to ask her name.

"I'm Tim Sparks," he said. "But everyone calls me Sparks." He surprised her by reaching out and shaking her hand. He had big hands and a powerful

26

handshake. He didn't seem to know his own strength.

"Hi, Sparks," Chelsea said, managing a smile.

Chelsea refilled the coffee cups for the three men at the other end of the counter. Then she checked Sparks's order. Not ready yet. She drew him a Coke from the dispenser on the counter and brought it to him.

"I just moved here," he said, spinning the glass between his hands, staring at her again. "To the Old Village."

"I just moved to Shadyside about a month ago," Chelsea said.

The two teenagers in the booth were signaling for a check.

"Is this town as nowhere as it looks?" Sparks asked, his lips forming a sneer.

"Yeah. I guess," Chelsea said.

Talking with this boy was making her feel really uncomfortable. Despite his jokes, there was something hard about him, something cold, something —dangerous.

"Hey—how about going to a movie with me?" he asked.

27

chapter

4

"*H*uh?"

"Come on, let's do something wild!" he urged.

Chelsea stared at Sparks, her mouth open. The question had been so unexpected, she found herself completely tongue-tied.

Sparks was looking across the counter at her expectantly.

Just then Chelsea felt a hand on her shoulder. She turned to see her father directly behind her, his forehead dotted with perspiration, an angry expression on his face.

"Those kids in the booth are waiting for their check," he said, speaking in a low voice, slowly and distinctly the way he did when he was trying to control his temper.

"Sorry," Chelsea said, pulling the check pad out of her apron pocket.

She glanced at Sparks. To her surprise, his face was bright red, and his dark eyes glowed with anger. He flashed a furious glance at Mr. Richards, then pushed himself up from the counter stool and quickly strode to the doorway.

"Hey—your hamburger!" Chelsea called after him.

He was gone. The door slammed hard behind him.

That was weird. Did he really ask me out? Chelsea thought.

Why did he run away? I guess he got mad because Dad interrupted us.

Wow.

She scribbled out the check and dropped it onto the table, thinking about Sparks.

So much for my first date, she thought regretfully.

She started to feel sorry for herself but forced her thoughts to the bright side. At least he asked me out. A boy actually asked me out on a date.

But would she have said yes? Would she have gone out with him?

He was so tough looking. Something about him seemed so old, so hard.

She thought about how angry Sparks had become when her father stopped their conversation, how his face had grown so—hateful.

No, Chelsea decided. I wouldn't have gone out with him.

No way.

I would've said no.

If I'd had the chance.

She glanced through the window into the kitchen. Her dad was tossing the burned hamburger into the trash, a sullen expression on his face.

Two more elderly customers came in—regulars. They took their usual booth by the window.

Chelsea brought them menus and stood by, hands shoved in her apron pockets, waiting for them to decide. She found her thoughts drifting to Will Blakely.

Staring out the window into the graying evening, she rehearsed her conversation with Will again. She knew every word by heart. She wondered if Will would say the things she had planned for him.

She wondered if Will would ever ask her to go to the movies.

Will *you* be my first date, Will?

Or will you walk away just as Sparks did?

Will seemed so shy, so painfully shy.

As shy as Chelsea.

Maybe *I'll* ask *him* out, Chelsea thought.

The idea excited her. It opened up a whole new world of possibilities.

She decided to forget the conversation she'd been

rehearsing. Instead, she'd ask him out for Saturday night.

No. No way, she immediately decided.

I could never do that. Never. I'd die. I'd die first.

What if he said no?

I'd be embarrassed for life.

Rehearsing how she might ask Will out, imagining their conversation, carried her through the rest of her shift. Seven o'clock, closing time, came quickly for her.

"Let's go home," her dad said brightly, emptying the cash register. He carefully placed all the money into a manila envelope, which he kept locked in the desk in a back room until he could take it to the bank the next morning.

"Mom won't be there," Chelsea told him.

"I know. She's working the late shift tonight," he replied with a helpless shrug.

Chelsea impatiently pulled off the apron she hated, bundled it up, and shoved it into the laundry bag. Her father went to lock the front door.

She heard noise at the front of the restaurant, shouts and feet scuffling.

Uttering a silent gasp, Chelsea focused her eyes on the door and saw three tough-looking young men, dressed in jeans and denim jackets, push their way in past her father.

She started to cry out, but her voice caught in her throat.

"We're closed!" Mr. Richards was shouting. "You don't belong in here. We're closed!"

One of the young men, tall and muscular with long, stringy blond hair, shoved her father back against the counter. "Empty the cash register and we'll get out," he snarled.

"There's nothing in there," Mr. Richards insisted, his eyes wide with fear. "Nothing!"

"He's telling the truth!" Chelsea managed to cry. She was huddled in the doorway to the kitchen.

"Let's just see," one of them said. He started to the cash register.

"No!" Chelsea's father screamed. "Get away! Get away from there!" He bolted after the young man and grabbed his shoulders from behind.

"No—Dad! Don't!" Chelsea screamed. "Dad—look out!"

chapter

5

Mr. Richards's eyes opened wide and he uttered a groan as one of the young men, a pale, skinny boy with wild gray eyes, stepped up behind him and brought a heavy pipe down on his head.

Chelsea screamed. And screamed again.

Her father's eyes rolled up in his head, his head wobbled on his neck, and he slumped to the floor as if in slow motion, landing first on his knees, then toppling face forward onto the linoleum.

He didn't move.

Chelsea's hands went up to her face, gripped her hair, and tugged. She tried to scream again, but no sound came out. "Dad—" she finally managed to cry. "Dad—"

The tall young man with the stringy blond hair slammed his fist hard against the front of the cash register when he saw that it was empty. "Let's get out of here!" he shouted to his friends.

"Dad—" Chelsea cried, staring down at her unmoving father, sprawled facedown on the floor, his arms folded under his body.

"Is he dead?" the one who hit him asked, dropping the section of pipe to the floor.

"You want to stick around to find out?" the blond one snapped.

All three of them were laughing as they ran out the front door. Chelsea watched them through the window as they disappeared around the corner.

She realized she was still tugging at her hair. Forcing her hands down, she dropped to the floor beside her father. "Dad—? Dad—?"

He didn't respond. She gasped as she saw bright red blood oozing from a deep gash on the crown of his head, the blood darkening as it ran through his thinning hair.

"Dad—?"

She rolled him over on his back.

Please be alive. Please be alive. Please be alive.

His eyes were closed. He was breathing slowly, noisily through his mouth. Each breath sounded like a groan.

Relieved that he was still alive, but alarmed by the dark blood puddling under his head, Chelsea pulled herself to her feet, stumbled to the phone in the kitchen, and dialed 911.

Two hours later Chelsea was home alone, pacing the living-room floor, her sneakers scraping the threadbare carpet, her arms crossed protectively over her chest. The floorboards creaked as she walked over them. The sound of the white enamel clock over the mantel seemed to grow louder with each tick.

Calm down, Chelsea, she told herself. Calm down. Calm down.

She repeated the words in her mind until they no longer made sense.

Everything's going to be okay, she thought.

Her father was in the intensive care unit of Shadyside General. The doctor told her he was in "serious but stable" condition.

She was too frightened and yet too relieved to ask what that meant.

Serious but stable.

Those words sounded better than *dead.*

"We don't detect any internal bleeding," the doctor, who had red hair and freckles and seemed about Chelsea's age, told her. "Your father was lucky."

Lucky? How was he lucky? Chelsea was about to say.

But she restrained herself, held in her bitterness,

forced a smile, and muttered some kind of polite answer.

Her mother had arrived at the hospital a few minutes later in her starched white uniform. She was pale and very frightened. The redheaded doctor had led her down the long, green-painted corridor, his hand on her shoulder, talking softly to her.

Now it was nearly ten o'clock, and Mrs. Richards was still at the hospital. From there she'd probably go back to work.

Chelsea was alone. Pacing the living room. The floorboards creaked eerily beneath her as if crying out from every step she took.

I hate this creepy old house, she thought, dropping into the worn corduroy armchair in the corner.

I hate this house. I hate this town.

I hate . . . everything.

Her anger couldn't chase away her fear.

The feeling of panic crept up on her, as if someone were pulling a heavy blanket over her, tightening it around her, smothering her under it.

What if Dad dies?

What will happen to us then?

Stop it, Chelsea, she scolded herself.

Stop it—right now.

She looked down and realized she had the phone in her hand. Without thinking, she punched in Nina's number.

36

The phone rang three times. Nina answered. "Hello?"

"Nina, it's me—Chelsea."

"Oh, hi. How are you doing? Doug and I were just—"

"Nina, something terrible happened," Chelsea interrupted impatiently, feeling the panic, feeling chilled all over, feeling her heart pound. "The restaurant was robbed. They hit my dad over the head."

"Oh, that's terrible!" Nina exclaimed. "Is he okay?" Chelsea could hear Doug in the background, asking what was going on.

"I'm not really sure. He's in intensive care. They say he's stable. My mom's at the hospital. I'm all alone here," Chelsea said, staring at the clock over the mantel until it became a white blur. "Could you do me a favor, Nina? Could you come and stay here tonight?"

"Sure. No problem," Nina said quickly. "I think it'll be okay. Let me ask my mom."

Chelsea heard the phone being put down, heard voices in the background but couldn't make out their words. Still staring at the clock, she waited and drummed her fingers on the soft arm of the big old chair.

"Be right over," Nina said.

"Thanks," Chelsea replied gratefully and hung up.

A few minutes later Chelsea saw car headlights in the driveway. She eagerly pulled open the front door and turned on the porch light.

This is really nice of Nina, Chelsea thought, peering out at the driveway through the storm door. She's a true friend.

Then she saw that Doug had come too.

Nina stepped into the hallway accompanied by a burst of cold air. She threw her arms around Chelsea, startling her, and gave her a hug. "Are you okay? You must have been so frightened!"

"Yes. I—" Chelsea suddenly couldn't find the words.

Doug pushed his way past them, rubbing his hands. "It got so cold," he said, peering curiously into the living room.

"I'll make some hot chocolate," Chelsea offered.

"Coffee would be better," he said, tossing his down jacket onto the floor in front of the couch.

"Okay. Coffee," Chelsea replied.

Doug and Nina followed her into the kitchen. "I'll make instant, okay?"

"Let me do it," Nina insisted. "You poor thing. Look—your hands are shaking."

"It—it was really scary," Chelsea admitted, stepping back and letting Nina fill the kettle. "I thought Dad was— I mean, there was so much blood."

"Who *were* these guys?" Doug asked, hoisting his large body onto a tall kitchen stool and leaning forward to rest his elbows on the counter.

"I don't know," Chelsea replied. "I never saw them before. They were all wearing denim jackets. Tough looking. Sort of like a gang."

"My dad says there's an awful lot of crime in the Old Village," Nina said thoughtfully.

"Is your dad going to be okay?" Doug asked.

"I think so," Chelsea said, suddenly afraid again, barely able to choke out the words.

A few minutes later they were back in the living room, the TV on, rapid-fire images of an MTV video filling the room with color. Chelsea sat in the corduroy armchair in the corner, her legs tucked under her, the coffee mug between her hands. Nina and Doug were on the couch.

Chelsea turned her eyes from the TV and saw Doug pull Nina close to him. She raised her face to his, and they kissed, a long, lingering kiss.

That's why Nina was so eager to leave home and come over here, Chelsea thought bitterly. So she and Doug would have a place to make out.

The two of them kissed again, as if they were alone in their own world, as if Chelsea weren't in the room.

She tried to watch the flickering images of the music video, but her eyes kept returning to Nina and Doug.

Watching them, she felt even more alone than before.

Why isn't that *me* with a guy on the couch? she asked herself. Why do I have to be the one by myself in the corner?

I'm so tired of being lonely, she thought.

I'm so tired of never going out, of never being with a boy, of never having a boy care about me.

Then she thought, If that tough-looking boy who came into the restaurant—Tim Sparks—yeah, if Sparks comes back and asks me out, I'll say yes. I won't hesitate for a second.

Chelsea closed her eyes.

She pictured her father being hit over the head again. She pictured the surprise on his face, the way his eyes rolled back in his head, the way he slumped to his knees, then fell forward. She pictured the blood gushing from the top of his head.

A frightening thought flashed into her mind just then. A thought about Sparks.

He had left so suddenly. Without even eating his hamburger.

He left as soon as he saw Chelsea's father.

As soon as he saw that Chelsea and her father were the only ones working in the restaurant.

What if Sparks was sent ahead to check out the place for the other three guys?

That would explain why he hurried out so quickly. And why the kids had appeared a short while later.

It can't be possible—*can* it? Chelsea asked herself.

Well, if he *is* one of them, he'll never come back.

He knows if he comes back, he could be caught.

Her mind spun faster than the images of the MTV video. She suddenly felt as if her brain were about to burst. She shut her eyes tight, the sound of the video throbbing in her ears.

What if he *does* come back?

What will I do?

chapter
6

_I_t was cold by the river, but pretty.

He liked cold weather. He liked the sharpness of wind that cut right through him. He liked the heaviness of it in his nostrils and against his forehead.

The morning sun was still low over the trees. Droplets of cold water clung to the shock of curly black hair protruding from under his wool ski cap. The wind gusted past him, then calmed.

The river was wider than he had imagined. He liked the cold, trickling sound it made as it moved past. Standing in the tall grass, he stared motionless into the bubbling brown waters for a long time, his hands jammed into his jeans pockets.

The wind swirled and returned to blow the grass almost flat against his ankles. It felt good. Good against his face too. His face was burning, burning. He needed the wind to cool it.

The river was called the Conononka. That's what the sign had said. It was probably an Indian name. What did it mean? Small, muddy river?

He chuckled to himself.

Across the river, wooded cliffs rose. He could see a road winding up them to the top. River Road it was called. He had read his map, studied it carefully.

He pulled off the wool ski cap and jammed it into his jacket pocket. It was keeping him warm. He wanted to feel cold. Especially his face. His face always felt so hot, as if he were under a burning sun, as if he were sunburned. The air was so cold, so sharp. But still it didn't cool his face.

He started walking again through the tall grass, his boots making squishing sounds in the soft ground, his cuffs soaked through from the morning dew.

Shadyside wasn't a bad town, he decided.

He'd made a good choice.

It was a pretty town, for the most part. And the river was nice.

He liked looking at the big houses in North Hills with their big, clean front yards, their tall hedges and perfectly trimmed evergreens. Of course, he could never fit in there. He didn't belong, and he knew it.

He liked the Old Village too, a more friendly part of Shadyside, more comfortable, more familiar.

Not a bad town, he thought, picking up a large, flat pebble from near the shore and trying to skip it across the rapidly flowing water.

It sank out of sight.

Of course, there were girls in this town who needed to die.

Girls just like you, Mom, he thought, jamming his hands back into his pockets.

He felt the anger begin again.

It always started in his stomach, then worked its way up his back until his neck muscles tightened. Then his head started to throb, throb with pain, throb from the anger.

And his face felt so hot, so burning hot.

The cold, trickling water, the cool, gusting wind, the damp, swaying grass at his feet—none of it helped.

None of it could stop the anger once it started.

And once he started thinking about his mother, the anger always came.

Some girls need to die, Mom. Just like you.

He had felt the anger for so many years. Since he was four.

Since his parents divorced.

Since his mother went away and took his big sister to live with her.

Since he was left with his father.

You knew what you were doing, Mom, he thought, heaving another stone into the river, heaving it with all his might, with all his anger, not trying to make it skip, trying to bury it deep, deep in the murky, brown waters.

You knew what you were doing.

You knew that Dad got drunk every night. You knew that Dad beat me when he got drunk.

But still you took my sister and ran. You left me behind. You left me with—him.

Every night I thought of you, Mom.

Every beating, I thought of you.

I thought only of you. And of my revenge.

I'm going to pay you back, Mom. I've already started to pay you back. In every town I visit.

If only I could find you. If only I knew where you lived.

A white kitten suddenly appeared at the edge of the trees. It stared across the grass at him with bold, black eyes.

"Here, kitty," he called, bending down and motioning with his hands. "Here, kitty, kitty."

The kitten stared back, tilted its head, but didn't move.

Sometimes I get my revenge, Mom, he thought, squatting down, motioning to the timid, white puffball. And it makes me feel better.

It makes me feel better to kill.

For a while.

"Here, kitty, kitty." He made clicking noises with his tongue and teeth. "Come here, kitty."

It has to be the right girl, Mom.

It can't be any girl. It has to be the right girl.

And I've found the right girl here in Shadyside.

She's dark like you, Mom.

At least, that's how I remember you.

I don't have a picture of you. You never sent me a picture. Or a letter.

You just left me behind to be beaten every night.

But I think she looks like you. She's dark and kind of chubby.

She's not real pretty, but she's okay.

And she seems so shy.

So perfectly shy.

She's right, Mom. I think she's just right.

When the anger comes again, I think she'll do fine.

"Here, kitty, kitty," he called.

The kitten took a reluctant step toward him, mewing softly. Then another step. Then another, staring at him, studying him warily.

"Here, kitty, kitty," he said in a soft, high voice. "I won't make you suffer long."

He picked up the kitten by the neck and strangled it.

chapter
7

Chelsea mopped the counter half-heartedly with a wet cloth. She glanced through the open window into the kitchen. No one there. Ernie, the brawny, tattooed fry cook, must have stepped out back for a smoke.

I hate working here without Dad around, Chelsea thought. Come to think of it, I hated working here when he *was* around. She sighed. At least the job paid her enough for some new clothes and an occasional CD.

After four days Mr. Richards was still in intensive care at Shadyside General, but the doctors were encouraged by his progress. Chelsea glanced up at the pink-and-blue neon clock. Twenty to seven, nearly closing time. If she hurried, she'd be able to see her dad at the hospital before visiting hours ended at seven-thirty.

She let her eyes roam slowly over the empty coffee shop. It was kind of scary being alone in there. What if those three creeps came back?

"Hey—Ernie?" she called, suddenly frightened. Ernie was big and very tough looking. He'd protect her if there was any trouble. But where *was* he?

"Ernie?"

No reply. He must still be back in the alley, she realized.

The big stainless-steel refrigerator clicked on loudly, startling her. She decided to think about Will, the new guy at school, to help pass the time.

So far, neither she nor Will had managed to get a real conversation going. Chelsea had rehearsed and rehearsed what she was going to say to him. She had imagined countless conversations, playing both parts in her mind.

In her mind their conversations were easy and fun. They kidded each other and laughed at each other's jokes.

But when she was actually sitting beside him in homeroom in the morning, she panicked. Or Mr. Carter had a full page of announcements to read. Or Will was busily writing in a notebook. Or it just didn't seem to be the right time.

He had smiled at her several times, and even said good morning twice and asked how she was doing. But then he returned to his notebook or a book he was reading.

He's *never* going to ask me out, Chelsea thought dispiritedly.

Despite this slow start to their relationship, she found herself thinking about him a lot. Even while practicing the saxophone, she sometimes pictured his shy smile, his dark, soulful eyes.

She was imagining a conversation with him when the door swung open and two tough teenagers swaggered in, their eyes nervously surveying the empty restaurant.

One of them was big and wide, with his blond hair shaved so close to his head it was like peach fuzz. The other was lean and lanky with a pock-marked face and an unpleasant grin. Both were wearing faded jeans and, despite the autumn cold, only T-shirts with the names of heavy metal groups emblazoned across the fronts.

Gripped with sudden fear, Chelsea stepped back from the counter, edging her way to the kitchen. "Ernie?" she called in a frightened whisper.

No reply.

I can't believe we're being robbed again, she thought, her back against the wall, her eyes searching the two thugs, trying to determine if they were carrying weapons.

The cash register contained less than fifty dollars, she knew. They're not going to hurt me for that amount of money, are they?

She decided she'd give them the money, hand it over without a word of protest.

Once again she pictured her father arguing with the three toughs just days before, trying to fend them off, trying to block their way to the cash register.

If he hadn't resisted, if he hadn't tried to fight them, if he hadn't tried to block their way to the cash register, they probably wouldn't have hit him, Chelsea told herself.

I'm not going to be brave, Chelsea decided. I'm going to be as cooperative as I can.

Having made certain that the coffee shop was deserted, the two young men stepped up to the cash register. "You all alone here?" the lean one asked Chelsea, his grin in place but his eyes tense.

"No," Chelsea said, trying to keep her voice steady. "I'm not alone."

The two creeps exchanged glances and laughed.

"We're just about to close up now," Chelsea said, her voice trembling despite her determination not to sound frightened. She raised her eyes to the clock. Ten to seven.

"Just about?" the skinny one asked.

They laughed again.

"What can I get you?" Chelsea asked.

"You're kind of cute in a way," the big one said, scratching his fuzzy blond head. His partner's grin grew wider.

"Really. We're closing now," Chelsea said, feeling her throat tighten. Her mouth felt dry as cotton.

"Yeah. You're the cutest thing in here," the big one said, resting a meaty hand on the counter just a few inches from the cash register. He stared into her eyes, waiting for her to react.

"What do you want?" Chelsea asked, more of a plea than a question.

"Well . . ." the big one started. Then he and his partner exchanged glances and giggled again.

Chelsea's heart thudded in her chest. If they're going to rob me, why don't they just do it and get it over with? she thought impatiently.

"Well, what do we want?" the big one asked, smirking at Chelsea.

"Good question," his partner added.

"What time did you say you get off work?" the big one asked, leaning over the counter, his face close to Chelsea's.

Her terror choked her.

What are they going to do?

Aren't they going to rob the store and leave?

Why are they asking me these questions? Why are they grinning at me like that?

"When do you get off?" the big one repeated.

Chelsea stared up at the clock. She opened her mouth to say something, to tell them to leave, to get out, to stop frightening her.

Before she could utter a sound, the door swung

open and another boy stepped into the brightly lit restaurant.

He walked quickly up the narrow aisle beside the counter, his hands at his sides. It took Chelsea a minute to recognize him. She had seen him only once before.

"Sparks!" she cried.

Then she hesitated.

Is Sparks with *them?* she wondered.

No.

The two toughs reacted with surprise as Sparks made his way into the restaurant. He stopped at the end of the counter and stared back at them, his powerful-looking arms tensed, his hands at his sides, his dark eyes staring from one to the other.

"You still open?" Sparks asked Chelsea.

"Just closing," Chelsea replied softly. She didn't move.

"Can I get a cup of coffee?" Sparks asked, staring at the two toughs.

"Okay," Chelsea said. She stepped toward the coffee machine.

"Later," the big guy said. He and his partner exchanged glances. Chelsea noticed that the smile had finally faded from the lean one's face.

"Yeah. Later," the lean one said, trying to make the words sound menacing.

They turned and ambled slowly past Sparks and out the restaurant.

Chelsea didn't move until the door had closed behind them. She breathed a loud sigh of relief and collapsed against the counter as she watched them walk away.

"Were they holding you up?" Sparks asked. He had taken a seat on the counter stool at the far end.

"Yes. I mean, I don't know. I'm not sure," Chelsea said shakily. Holding the coffeepot over the white china cup, she struggled to keep her hand steady as the coffee splashed into the cup.

When she set the cup down in front of him on the counter, she noticed him studying her with his dark eyes, his expression serious and thoughtful.

She slid a small stainless-steel pitcher of milk toward him. "They were acting real tough. I don't know what they were going to do. Rob me, I guess."

She pulled off the apron and bundled it up. He took a sip of the coffee, black, his eyes still on her.

She tossed the rolled-up apron into the corner. "They seemed to be afraid of you," she said, smiling uneasily.

"They should be," Sparks replied. He stared down at the coffee cup.

What does he mean by that? Chelsea wondered. Is he making a joke? Or is he serious?

His expression didn't reveal any answer.

He took another sip of coffee, steam rising above his black hair, then quickly disappearing into the

• lights. "Dangerous around here," he said, still avoiding her eyes.

What was he trying to say? Was he just making a comment? Or was he trying to warn her?

Chelsea heard scraping sounds from the kitchen. She turned to see Ernie, the fry cook, cleaning off the grill, a stub of a cigarette stuck between his teeth. "Time to knock off?" he called out to her in his gruff rasp of a voice.

"Yeah," Chelsea told him. "I'll close up."

Sparks took a long sip of coffee. Chelsea waited for him to say something, but he appeared lost in thought.

She wanted to say something to him, to thank him for saving her from the two grinning toughs, to keep the conversation going. But her shyness interfered. She couldn't think of anything to say.

Is he going to ask me out again? she wondered.

If he does, will I say yes?

She realized she was frightened of him and drawn to him at the same time.

Why can't I think of anything to say? Why can't I just say *something?* Why is it so easy for other girls, girls like Nina, and so hard for me?

These questions flashed through her mind as she stared at him from behind the counter, her eyes studying his dark, serious face.

"Need a refill?" she asked, clearing her throat first.

He shook his head. "No. Thanks."

Ernie came out of the kitchen, his jacket slung over his muscular arm. "See you tomorrow," he said, giving her a little nod, then turning his eyes on Sparks.

"Okay. Bye," Chelsea said and watched Ernie go out the door.

I'm alone with Sparks now, she realized.

The thought sent a small, cold shiver down her back.

Sparks took a final sip of the coffee, pushed the cup away, and dropped a dollar onto the counter.

Is he going to say something? Chelsea wondered. Is he going to ask me out again?

I'll say yes, Sparks, she thought, trying to send brain waves from her mind to his. I'll say yes.

He pushed himself up, his big biceps bulging. Standing, he flashed her a shy smile. "Thanks."

"Welcome," she said, reaching for the cup.

"See you," he said. His sneakers moved silently over the linoleum floor. He left without looking back. The door closed quietly behind him.

Chelsea's shoulders slumped forward. She sighed, disappointed, and dropped the coffee cup into the dirty dish tray.

Her mind whirred. She felt terribly mixed up. As she made one final inspection, turning out the lights as she went, she realized she was disappointed. And relieved.

A few minutes later she stepped outside into a cold, clear night. She carefully locked the front door and pulled the metal grate across it, as she had seen her father do. Then she hurried to the hospital to see how he was doing.

A few blocks from the coffee shop, Sparks pulled open the door to his third-floor walkup apartment and stepped into the cramped living room without turning on any lights. Closing the door left him in near darkness; only pale yellow light drifted in through the window from a streetlight just below.

Pacing the small, hot room, he slammed a fist repeatedly into his open palm. After a few minutes he uttered an angry cry, continuing to pace like an agitated zoo animal.

Why didn't I ask her out? he asked himself.

Why didn't I do it? I wanted to. I *planned* to.

Why did I just sit there like a jerk, sipping that bitter coffee?

We were all alone. All alone.

Why did I blow this opportunity?

What's *wrong* with me?

Furious with himself, he jerked the phone off the table, pulled the cord out of the wall, and heaved the phone with all his might against the window.

The glass shattered noisily. But he couldn't hear it over the angry roar in his brain.

chapter
___
8

*T*he next day after school Chelsea slammed her locker shut and checked down the crowded, noisy corridor for Nina. It took her a while to spot her friend. A stray dog, a large German shepherd frantically waving its tail, had wandered into the school. A crowd had gathered around it, blocking the hallway. The dog was barking loudly, the sound echoing off the walls.

What's the big deal about a dog? Chelsea wondered. Everyone's acting as if it's the most exciting thing that ever happened!

A couple of kids were leading it to the principal's office, not an easy task since the dog had no collar. A crowd of kids followed behind it.

Finally Chelsea spotted Nina standing at her locker, her blue wool coat in her hands, staring back at her.

"Hey—Nina!" Chelsea made her way through the still-buzzing hall. She had decided to ask her friend's advice about Sparks and Will.

Mainly she wanted to ask, How can I get one of them to ask me out?

But to her surprise, Nina's expression was glum, her eyes red rimmed as if she'd been crying. "Hey—what's wrong?" Chelsea asked, slinging her backpack onto her other shoulder.

"It's that stupid Doug," Nina said angrily. She slammed her locker door shut, pushing it so hard the door bounced back open.

"What's with Doug?" Chelsea asked.

"I saw him at lunch," Nina replied unhappily, "talking with Suki Thomas."

"I don't know her," Chelsea said, turning her eyes up the hall where the big barking dog was fleeing the group of kids chasing after him. "But what's wrong with him talking to someone?"

"It's the *way* he was talking," Nina said, slamming her locker door again. This time it stayed shut.

Chelsea started to say something, but the dog came flying by just then, its paws sliding across the hard tile floor, its eyes wild and excited.

"Let it go! Open the door and let it go!" someone was yelling.

At the end of the hall someone pushed open the

double doors, and still slipping and sliding, the grateful dog bounded outside and disappeared.

A happy cheer rang through the hall. After a few more minutes of laughter and excited buzzing, kids pulled on their coats, picked up their books, and started to leave.

"I want to tell you about this boy who came into the restaurant a couple of times," Chelsea said, jostled by two guys in hockey uniforms, carrying hockey sticks, trying to squeeze past her.

Nina turned the combination lock on her locker, making sure it was locked, then she remembered a book she needed. With a frustrated groan she started turning the combination wheel again.

"He's sort of tough looking," Chelsea continued. "His name is Tim Sparks, but he says everyone calls him Sparks. He seems moody. I mean, sort of angry. But maybe he's just shy or something. The first time he came into the restaurant, he asked me out. But I didn't say anything. I mean, we were interrupted. By my dad. So then—"

"I just don't believe Doug," Nina interrupted. Her face was hidden by the open locker door. She was squatting down on her knees, searching for the book on the floor of the locker. "I mean, Suki Thomas is such a tramp."

"Anyway, I think he's kind of interesting," Chelsea continued. But then she stopped. She realized she was wasting her breath. "You haven't heard a word I said," she accused Nina.

Nina climbed to her feet and closed the locker door. "Huh?" She wrinkled her forehead in consternation. "Sorry, Chelsea. I was thinking about something else." And then her eyes grew wide. "Hey, there he is. Hey—Doug!" she called. "Doug, wait up!"

Struggling to shove her books into her backpack, she hurried down the hall to catch up with her boyfriend.

Feeling let down and disappointed, Chelsea stood staring after Nina for a while. Then she closed Nina's locker for her, made sure it was locked, and trudged toward the front door of the high school.

Nina's a good friend—when Doug isn't around, she thought unhappily. But when he's around, I'm invisible.

She was a few steps from the door when a hand touched her shoulder. Startled, she stopped abruptly and twisted back.

It was Will Blakely.

His cheeks were bright pink, and he was smiling shyly. His black hair was poking out from under a navy blue Dodgers cap. He was carrying a large looseleaf binder and one textbook under the arm of his black and tan wool jacket.

"Hi," he said, his smile growing wider.

"Oh. Hi," Chelsea replied. "How are you?"

He shrugged. "Okay."

"That's not a Shadyside jacket," Chelsea said, pointing.

What a dumb comment, she thought. Of *course* it's not a Shadyside jacket. Nothing like saying the obvious.

"It's—uh—from my old school."

"Where was that?" she asked, shifting her backpack on her shoulders.

"Down South," Will said, staring past her. "You doing anything?" He continued to avoid her eyes.

"I was just going home," Chelsea said. Two kids from their homeroom pushed past them, waving as they headed out the door. "I have to go to work in a couple of hours."

"Oh." His face filled with disappointment. "Then I guess you don't have time to take a walk."

"Oh. Sure. Sure, I do," Chelsea replied excitedly. "A walk would be nice. It's a pretty day."

She peered out through the doors as some kids opened them. Clouds had covered the sun. The sky was overcast and gray. "I guess it *was* a nice day," she said, giggling.

"Oh. You don't want to go?" he asked.

He's worse than I am, she thought.

That thought cheered her.

"Let's go," she said. "Shadyside Park is behind the school. Have you been there?"

He shook his head, then followed her toward the back of the building. They walked through the long corridors without saying a thing.

It was colder outside than Chelsea had thought. A gusting wind made it feel more like winter than autumn. She stopped to zip her jacket up to the collar. Then they walked side by side past the teacher parking lot, past the baseball and soccer fields, and into the broad, tree-filled park that stretched behind the school.

Chelsea took a deep breath. "The air smells so good," she said.

"Especially after breathing the air in school," he agreed. "I think it's recycled from 1920 or something."

She laughed. Hey, he has a sense of humor, she thought.

He laughed too, a dry, nearly silent laugh from deep in his throat.

He's really good-looking, she thought.

She raised her eyes to the trees. More leaves had fallen, making the branches wintery and bare. "You know, the woods beyond the park stretch all the way to the river," she said.

"I'd like to see the river," he said. "Is there a path through the woods?"

She nodded. "Yeah. I guess. I'm pretty new here myself, you know. We moved to Shadyside at the end of September."

"You move a lot?" he asked, his expression serious.

"No. Not really," she told him, her arm bumping against him as they headed through the grass, their sneakers crunching over brown leaves. "My dad had a chance to buy a restaurant here, so we came."

"You're rich?" he asked and then blushed. "I mean—"

She laughed, more at his embarrassment than at the question. "It's just a tiny coffee shop in the Old Village. And my dad had to take out a big loan to buy it. But it's something he's always wanted."

They walked in silence for a while.

"You move a lot?" Chelsea asked, trying hard to keep the conversation going.

"Yeah," he said with some bitterness. She waited for him to say more. But he got a faraway look in his eyes and, staring straight ahead, continued walking in silence.

They followed a narrow, leaf-covered path through the trees. The sky grew darker. It seemed to lower itself over them, darkening the woods.

"It's almost cold enough to snow," Chelsea said.

Oh, no. Stop it, she scolded herself. Don't talk about the weather.

"I like snow," he said, turning to grin at her. "It's so pure."

He stopped in front of a broad white birch tree and tossed his book and binder down at the foot of the smooth trunk. "Let's leave our stuff here," he suggested, gesturing toward her backpack. "That looks so heavy."

"Good idea." She pulled off the backpack and dropped it beside his stuff. "I feel a thousand pounds lighter."

"We'll come back this way," he said, lingering behind her a few paces as the path curved through the trees.

"Hey—I think I can see the river!" Chelsea exclaimed, pointing. "Look!"

She waited for him to catch up. "It's called the Conononka," she said.

He came up close beside her, smiling, his breath steaming in front of him. She decided she loved the way his dark eyes glowed every time he smiled.

I'm walking with a boy in the woods, she thought happily.

For most girls, that's probably no big deal.

But I've never walked alone with a boy in the woods before.

She smiled at Will for no reason in particular. He returned the smile, then quickly turned his eyes back to the path.

They walked a little farther. The air grew colder as they neared the riverbank. She could hear the rush of the water now, soft under the blowing wind.

"This walk was a good idea," she said brightly. "Hey—"

She realized he had fallen behind. Turning back, she saw that he had something in his hands. It was a length of gray cord. He had it doubled over and was pulling it taut, then loosening it as he walked.

He held it up when he saw her staring at it. "I just found this," he said, pointing down at a low shrub. "On the ground over there." He shrugged and stuffed it into his jacket pocket.

It started to snow, an early snow, the first snow of the year, giant white flakes filtering down through the trees. Chelsea opened her mouth and stuck out her tongue, hoping to catch a snowflake. But she pulled her tongue back in when she saw Will staring at her.

"Does it usually snow this early in October?" he asked.

"I don't know," she replied. "Probably." She glanced at her watch. "Oh. I'd better get home. I can't be late for work."

"Sorry," he said, his cheeks reddening. "I didn't mean to get you in trouble or anything."

"No," she protested, taking his arm as she struggled to step over a large fallen tree branch. "The walk was great. I enjoyed it." She smiled at him.

He didn't return the smile. His expression was troubled. He took off ahead of her with long strides.

The snow stopped as quickly as it had begun. The sky brightened a little.

When they reached their belongings at the birch

tree, he stopped suddenly and turned to face her. His dark eyes glowed. They seemed to burn into hers.

He hesitated. Then he asked, "Want to go to a movie or something Saturday night?"

"Yeah. Great!" Chelsea exclaimed. And then blurted out, "My first date!"

She immediately squeezed her eyes shut in embarrassment. She bent down and reached for her backpack, hoping against hope that he hadn't heard her say that, that he couldn't see how embarrassed she was now.

Why did she blurt that out?

Why did she always have to be so *uncool?*

I want to die, she thought. I just want to sink into the ground here and never be seen again.

Reluctantly she raised her eyes up to his. To her surprise, he was smiling at her warmly.

"Can you keep a secret, Chelsea?" he asked, coming close. "It's my first date too."

"I'm glad," she said awkwardly. She wished she could think of something better, more clever to say. But at least his confession made her feel less embarrassed.

"Let's make it a secret date," he suggested quietly, standing very close, staring into her eyes. "Don't tell anyone. Let's make it our private, secret date. Just for us."

That's so romantic, she thought.

She felt like leaping high in the air and shouting for joy.

A really good-looking boy had asked her out on a first date.

He was so nice.

And so—honest.

He was shy like she was. And he liked her.

"Okay," she said, her voice almost a whisper. "It'll be our secret, Will. Our secret first date."

chapter
9

The next afternoon as Chelsea was practicing her saxophone, the front door opened and her mother came bursting into the living room. Her hair was drenched, her raincoat soaked through.

Chelsea raised her eyes to the window and saw that it was as black as night outside and pouring rain. The snow of the day before had lasted only a few minutes, not long enough to stick. This afternoon Chelsea had been concentrating so hard on her music, she hadn't even been aware of the rainstorm.

"Mom—are you okay?" she cried, rushing across the room to help pull off her dripping raincoat. "Why are you home so early?" She glanced at the clock above the mantel. It was four-thirty.

"Don't ask," her mother replied wearily. She shivered and turned to Chelsea. "I'm chilled to the bone."

Chelsea gasped when she saw that her mother's white uniform was stained with dark red blood.

"Mom—what happened?" she cried.

"We had a little accident at the home," Mrs. Richards said. "One of the patients slipped in the bath and got cut. It looks much worse than it was. Only my spare uniform is here. Upstairs. I had to come all the way home in this downpour to get it."

"Then you're going back to work?" Chelsea asked, still holding the raincoat.

"Yes. I have to take Alice Brody's shift too. She has the flu." She headed up the stairs to her room to change. "Oh, look at my shoes. Soaked through, and they're my only pair."

Chelsea followed her to her room. "You're always at the nursing home, Mom. I never see you anymore."

"Chelsea, don't start complaining," her mother said sternly. "I'm not in the mood. Believe me." She stopped at the door to her room and turned around. "I'll be home Saturday night for dinner. I don't have to go to work until late that night. You and I can have a nice dinner together and chat."

"No, we can't," Chelsea said.

Her mother's expression changed to bewilderment.

"I have a date," Chelsea told her. "With a boy."

Mrs. Richards's eyes went wide. "Hey, that's great."

"No wisecrack?" Chelsea asked, finding herself a little disappointed that her mother hadn't cracked her usual sarcastic joke.

"I'm too wet for wisecracks," her mother said. "Besides, I'm happy for you. I know how lonely you've been."

As her mother changed into a clean uniform, Chelsea told her about Will, how he was the new boy in her homeroom, how they went for a walk in Shadyside Park, how he seemed shy but nice.

Mrs. Richards, pulling on the starched white skirt, appeared very pleased. "Can't wait to meet him," she told Chelsea, smiling. She straightened the skirt. "Oh, I almost forgot to tell you. I talked to your dad."

"And?"

"And he's out of intensive care. He's in a semi-private room. The doctors think he'll be able to come home in a week or two." She hurried over to Chelsea and gave her a quick, emotion-filled hug. "Isn't that great?"

"It sure is!" Chelsea exclaimed happily. "And that means we can visit him at regular visiting hours." She glanced at the clock on her mother's bedtable. "Oh, no! I'm going to be late for work.

I'm relieving Kristy tonight, and she really gets steamed if I'm two seconds late."

"Come on. Get your coat," Mrs. Richards said, staring into the dresser mirror and giving her hair two quick brushes before hurrying to the door. "I'll drop you off on my way."

The rain kept most customers away from the coffee shop. A few people straggled in, shaking the water off their coats, rubbing their hands, and shivering from the cold. It was a big night for soups, and chili, and steaming cups of coffee.

But Chelsea spent most of the time sitting in a booth in the back doing her geometry homework. She had nearly finished the last problem when a dark figure slid silently into the booth across the table from her.

"Sparks!" she cried, startled.

He grinned at her, water dripping from his black hair down his forehead. He pulled off his jacket and stuffed it beside him on the seat. He was wearing a faded blue workshirt under the jacket.

"How's it going?" he asked, shaking his head and sending a spray of water onto the table.

Chelsea closed her notebook. "Slow," she said. She felt a chill. He was staring at her so hard, so intensely. Her stomach suddenly felt fluttery, her throat tight. She glanced to the kitchen. Ernie was sitting on a stool near the sink, doing a crossword puzzle in a folded-up newspaper.

Chelsea slid out of the booth, eager to get away from his unblinking eyes. "What can I get you?"

"Coffee," he said, tapping his fingers rapidly on the tabletop. "And a doughnut if they're not too stale."

"They're from this morning, but I think they're okay," she told him.

Why does he make me so nervous? she asked herself as she dropped a doughnut onto a plate, then headed to the coffeepot. Is it because I'm attracted to him?

Or is it because there's something strange about him, strange and dangerous?

Does he like me? she wondered. She filled the cup too full. She tilted it and let some pour off the top.

No. He doesn't like me. It's not like I'm pretty or anything. Maybe he's really lonely. Or maybe he's just playing games. Maybe he's secretly laughing at me.

Yes, she decided bitterly. He's probably laughing at me.

She decided to try to find out more about him.

After setting the doughnut and coffee down, she slid back into the booth. He didn't look at all surprised. His expression was blank, unreadable. He took a big bite of the doughnut, flakes of sugar sticking to his lips.

"So where are you from?" Chelsea asked, trying to sound casual.

He chewed, then swallowed, then took a sip of coffee. "From around," he replied, his dark eyes gleaming.

"Where's that?" Chelsea asked.

He shrugged his broad shoulders. "Just around." He took another bite of the doughnut. "I move around a lot."

"You're not in school?" she asked, determined to get some information from him, *any* information.

"Yes," he replied quickly.

"Where?" Chelsea asked.

"Well, actually, no," he said, avoiding her stare. "Dropped out." He took another sip of coffee, gazing at her over the steaming cup. He grinned. "I'm a high school dropout."

She laughed uncomfortably. "School isn't so bad," she said. "I'm in the band."

She immediately regretted revealing that.

Why did I tell him that? she wondered, feeling her face grow hot. It sounds so dorky.

"What do you play?" he asked seriously. "Tuba?"

He didn't seem to be joking, but Chelsea was insulted. He thinks I'm so big and fat, I should be playing tuba. Why didn't he say *flute?*

She shook her head. "You're making fun of me," she said, turning her eyes to the kitchen. Ernie,

73

pencil poised over the folded-up newspaper, hadn't moved.

"No, I'm not!" he protested, raising both hands in the air. "I just thought maybe you play tuba."

"Well, I don't," she replied sharply. "I play saxophone."

"That was my second choice," he said, lowering his eyes to his coffee cup, a hint of a smile crossing his lips.

"So, do you work?" Chelsea asked, changing the subject.

"Do you like to ask questions?" he snapped, his smile fading.

"Sorry." Again, Chelsea felt her face grow hot. "Just curious. If you want me to go, I'll—"

He reached across the table suddenly and grabbed her arm. "No. Stay." He didn't seem to be aware of his own strength. His tight grasp was hurting Chelsea. She was about to protest when he let go and pulled his arm away.

"I'm looking for a job," he said, his expression a blank again. "My mom and dad, they want me to get a job. You know, until I decide what I want to do."

"Where have you looked?" Chelsea asked.

He let his eyes survey the empty coffee shop. "Well, this place looks pretty good," he said, his smile returning, his dark eyes gleaming. "Looks like you could use some extra help here. What do you say?"

Chelsea sighed. "Not funny. Where have you been looking?"

"Well, I had an interview at the mill," he said. "I think it went pretty well."

"The mill has been closed for years," Chelsea blurted out. "My friend Nina drove me up to see it."

"Oh. Then I guess the interview *didn't* go very well," he cracked and snickered at his own joke.

She had caught him in a lie.

Maybe, she thought, everything he says is a lie.

What is he trying to hide?

Suddenly he reached across the table again and touched her hand. "Hey—you busy Saturday night?" he asked. "Let's go do something wild."

I can't go out with him, Chelsea thought, realizing that her heart was pounding in her chest. I don't know anything about him.

And I don't trust him.

She suddenly remembered Will.

"I already have a date for Saturday night," she said.

Sparks stared at her as if trying to decide if she was telling the truth. "Too bad," he said finally, jumping to his feet.

Chelsea looked up at him. His features were tight with anger.

He reached into his jeans pocket, then tossed two rolled-up dollar bills onto the table in front of her.

His face was red. His eyes were narrowed, his lips drawn tight.

"See you," he said coldly.

"Yeah. Okay," Chelsea replied in a tiny voice she barely recognized.

He grabbed his jacket with an angry jerk, then turned and stomped toward the entrance. He pushed open the door and stepped out into the rain, still carrying his jacket.

"Wow," Chelsea said out loud, not moving from the booth.

What a scary guy, she thought.

Like a bomb ready to explode.

chapter
10

"Where are we going?" Chelsea asked.

"To the movies," Will replied quickly, his eyes straight ahead, both hands on top of the steering wheel.

"But the mall is that way," Chelsea told him, pointing, "on Division Street."

"I know," he said softly. He pushed down on the gas pedal, and the old Pontiac responded with a roar. "The same film is playing in Waynesbridge. I saw it in the paper."

Chelsea stared out the car window, hiding her disappointment. This was her first date, after all. She wanted to go to the sixplex at the mall where all the Shadyside High kids hung out, where everyone would see her with Will.

Why was he taking her to the movies in the next town?

She stared out at the houses passing in the darkness. The radio was turned to an oldies station, and a Beach Boys song filled the car.

The rain had finally stopped that afternoon. It was a clear, cool Saturday night; the grass and trees, even the street, were sparkling from the recent rain.

Even in the dark everything seems much cleaner, much brighter, Chelsea thought. Was it because of the rain? Or because she was out on her first date?

Suddenly she realized why Will was taking her to Waynesbridge.

It was their first *secret* date. He was keeping it their secret.

Their private, romantic secret.

She turned and smiled at him, watching his serious expression as he drove, feeling better, feeling nervous and happy at the same time.

"This is a great car," she said, running her hand on the vinyl seat. "How old is it?"

"I'm not sure," he replied. "Late seventies, I guess."

"Did your family buy it when it was new?" Chelsea asked.

"Yeah . . . uh-huh. It's the only car I've ever driven," he said.

"You'd better put on the defroster, don't you

think?" Chelsea asked. "The windshield is getting all steamy."

He slowed to let a car pass, then reached his right hand to the dashboard and fumbled around with the dials, trying to slide on the defroster. Chelsea laughed as he turned on the air conditioner instead.

She stopped laughing when a disturbing thought flashed into her mind. If his family has had this car most of his life, why doesn't he know how to work the defroster?

"How come you can't work the defroster?" The question just slipped out of her mouth. "I mean, you said this was the only car you've ever driven."

In the light of the passing streetlights she could see his cheeks go red. He slowed the car a little, his eyes straight ahead on the road.

"I guess you found out my secret," he said quietly, seriously.

She felt a sudden stab of dread. "Your secret?"

"Yeah," he said, glancing at her for a split second. "I'm a complete klutz."

He laughed and slapped the steering wheel with his right hand. She laughed too, mostly from relief.

"I was hoping you wouldn't find out my deep, dark secret," he said. "At least not so early on our first date. But it's true. I'm a complete klutz. I can't even turn on a defroster."

"I'm a klutz too," Chelsea admitted. She told

him about the time her saxophone case had come open just before a band concert at her old school, and her mouthpiece and another section fell off the stage, and she had to climb down and get them in front of the entire school.

"That's pretty klutzy," he said. "But at least you can work a defroster."

They told each other stories about their klutziness the rest of the way to the movie theater. It was the easiest, most relaxed conversation they'd had.

He has a great sense of humor, Chelsea thought. She wondered if he liked her.

He seemed to. He seemed looser, more relaxed than he ever had with her before.

"There's a parking place," he said and backed the car in easily. He cut the engine and the lights, pocketed the car key, and pushed open his door.

As the ceiling light came on, Chelsea saw that Will had left his wallet on the seat. "Hey—" she called to him, picking up the wallet.

He grabbed it from her so quickly and with such force that he frightened her. "Sorry," he said, frowning down at her. "Didn't mean to startle you." He jammed the wallet into the back pocket of his jeans and slammed his door shut.

What was *that* all about? Chelsea wondered, pushing open her door and climbing out.

He didn't think I was going to take his wallet, did he? That's ridiculous.

She forgot the whole incident as Will, smiling warmly at her, put a hand on her shoulder and guided her toward the movie theater.

The movie, a comedy with Will Ferrell and at least two Quaid brothers, was actually pretty funny. Chelsea usually didn't enjoy that kind of film, but sitting so close to Will, out on her first date, feeling happy, she found herself laughing a lot, and even sorry when the final car chase came to a crashing end and the houselights came up.

The night was surprisingly warm as they made their way out of the theater. A sliver of a moon hovered above, cut in half by a thread of a black cloud.

"That was pretty dumb," Will said, smiling, his hand resting gently on her shoulder as they walked to the car.

"Yeah, but it was funny," she replied.

"Hungry?" he asked.

She shrugged.

"Know what I'd like to do?" He stopped beside the car and stood close to her on the sidewalk, his dark eyes glowing excitedly in the light from a streetlight.

"What?"

"Drive around, then park somewhere and talk,"

he said, staring into her eyes. He shoved his hands into his jacket pockets.

"That sounds great," Chelsea said.

"Do you know a good place to go?" Will asked, glancing down the street, which was rapidly emptying as cars drove away from the theater.

"You mean you don't go parking with girls every week?" Chelsea teased.

He chuckled. "I'm new here, remember," he said. "Give me a break."

"Well, I'm new too," she said. "But I guess we could go to River Ridge. That's a place on the cliffs above the river. Nina said kids go up there a lot."

"Who's Nina?" he asked, sounding suspicious.

"My friend," Chelsea told him. "She's just about the only friend I've made so far in Shadyside," and then she shyly added, "except for you."

Instead of acting pleased, he frowned. "Did you tell Nina about our date?"

"No, of course not," Chelsea said. She pulled open the passenger door. "It's our secret, remember?"

She smiled up at him and his expression relaxed. "Of course I remember."

He walked around the front of the car, opened his door, and slid in behind the wheel. A minute later they were driving back toward Shadyside, silently, comfortably, the radio playing softly in the rear speakers.

"How do you get to River Ridge?" Will asked as they neared town. Then he answered his own question. "I guess you take River Road."

"I guess," Chelsea replied. "Oh. I love this song. The Temptations." She sang along to "My Girl" for a few seconds. "Do you always listen to an oldies station, Will?"

He didn't reply. He stared straight ahead through the windshield, but his thoughts seemed to be a million miles away.

"Will?" She touched his arm.

"Oh." He shook his head. "Sorry. I was thinking about something. This is a great song, isn't it?"

River Ridge may have been a popular parking spot for Shadyside High kids during the summer, but on this October night, it was completely deserted.

Will pulled the car right up to the cliff edge and cut the headlights. Below, the river flowed, black and silent. Just across the river stretched the town of Shadyside, mostly dark except for a few twinkling lights from houses and an occasional blinking traffic light.

Chelsea could feel her heart racing. Her entire body was tingling. She felt so happy. She felt like singing, or maybe throwing open the door and flying out of the car, flying over the cliff, over the river, into the dark, starry sky to soar over the small, twinkling town so far below.

Will dropped his hands from the steering wheel and turned to her, smiling. He slid one arm behind her on the back of her seat.

He's going to kiss me, she thought happily.

I'm up here on River Ridge, parked with a boy who likes me.

My first date, she thought, smiling back at Will, leaning toward him as he pulled her close. My first, secret date.

She licked her lips. They felt so dry. But before she could finish, his lips were pushing against hers.

The kiss was awkward and brief.

But he was smiling as he pulled his head back. "Nice night," he said.

Chelsea nodded. She wanted the kiss to last longer. She wanted him to kiss her again, to hold her.

She had fantasized about a night like this so many times.

She wanted it to be just like all her fantasies.

But Will removed his arm from behind her and replaced it on the wheel. "Feel like taking a walk?" he asked softly. "A short one. It's so pretty up here. I like looking at the town, don't you?"

He pushed open his car door without waiting for her reply.

Chelsea pushed her door open too. He's so romantic, she thought. He was always so shy in school. But up there, he seemed more confident, more self-assured.

Maybe it's because he's starting to feel comfortable with me, Chelsea thought.

She forced herself to calm down. The light in the car went out as she closed the car door behind her. The night grew much darker.

"Will?" For a moment she couldn't find him. Then, as her eyes adjusted, she saw him standing at the cliff edge, his hands in his jacket pockets, staring over at the town.

"Look," he said, turning back to her and motioning for her to come stand beside him. "It doesn't look real. It's like a miniature town from up here."

She took a few steps but hesitated several feet behind him.

"Come on over," he called impatiently.

Chelsea took another step, then stopped. "I can't," she told him. "I'm afraid of heights."

For the tiniest fraction of a second, disappointment crossed his face. It quickly disappeared when he hurried back to her and put his arm around her shoulders.

"I'm sorry. I didn't know," he apologized, guiding her away from the cliff toward the woods behind the road. "We'll walk this way," he said softly. "I like the woods at night too, don't you?"

"It's a little cold," she said with a shiver, her

breath steaming in front of her, white against the black night. "But I like it," she added quickly. "It's so peaceful up here. I feel as if I'm a million miles away from home."

Their sneakers scraped against the hard dirt path that led to the woods. As they made their way under the first trees, it became even darker. There was no light now, not even moonlight.

Will slowed his pace, let Chelsea get a few steps ahead. Then he pulled the length of cord from his jacket pocket, silently untangled it, and pulled it taut between his hands with a quick *snap.*

chapter
11

As Will readied the cord between his hands and hurried to catch up to Chelsea, he thought about his sister.

Chelsea was so much like Jennifer.

Or at least the way he remembered Jennifer.

You were the lucky one, Jennifer, he thought. You went with Mom.

You didn't get the drunken beatings night after night. You didn't live in a horror show you couldn't escape from.

You and Mom had it nice. You ran away and left me. You didn't tell me where you were going.

You didn't write to me. You didn't call.

You and Mom had such a good life.

And you never even thought about me.

Well, I've been thinking about *you,* Jennifer. I've been thinking about you and Mom a lot.

A lot of girls deserve to die because of you.

A lot of girls are going to die.

And then someday I'm going to find you two.

And you're both going to die.

Just as I died every night. Every night.

Just as I wished I were dead.

He opened his mouth and sucked in a cold lungful of air.

Holding his breath, he stepped up behind Chelsea and raised the length of cord, ready to lower it around her neck.

chapter

12

*T*he twin lights startled them both.

Will had just enough time to jam the cord back into his jacket pocket as Chelsea spun around. "What's that?" she cried, her voice a whisper.

Car headlights.

Another car was pulling in beside theirs.

"The lights—they scared me," Chelsea said, holding on to his arm. "We were so alone and—"

"It's getting too crowded up here," he said, laughing a bit too loudly. "Let's go." He took her hand, leading the way quickly back to the car.

His heart was pounding. When he saw the headlights, his first thought was that it was a patrol car out searching for the old Pontiac he had stolen earlier that afternoon.

But it wasn't the police. It was just two teenagers looking for a place to make out.

They had ruined his plans, ruined his night.

He'd have to take her home and then dump the car.

He'd have to kill her another night.

Be patient, he told himself, holding open the passenger door for her, forcing a warm, reassuring smile on his face.

Be patient. There will be other nights.

This girl's time will come.

Soon.

He started up the car and backed onto the road. Then he switched on the headlights, the thick woods lighting up in front of them.

Chelsea shivered, shoving her hands into her coat pockets. "That was nice," she said dreamily, sliding down low, resting her head against the back of the seat. "It's so beautiful up here."

"Yeah," Will agreed, eyes straight ahead on the road.

She realized she'd never felt this happy. Even at her old school, she had been an outsider, always the lonely girl, the one who stayed home watching TV on Saturday nights while her friends went to parties and out on dates.

"Why don't you do something with your hair?" her friends would insist.

Or: "Why don't you lose a little weight?"

Or: "Why don't you wear something a little sexier, a little more daring?"

Everyone always had plenty of advice for Chelsea.

But now she didn't need their advice. Now she was out on a date with a boy who really liked her. With a boy who kissed her and took her on a romantic walk high above the river, high above the town.

Feeling so happy, feeling so comfortable, she leaned against him and whispered, "Why don't we go to my house?"

He didn't react immediately. He seemed to be lost in thought, far away somewhere.

For a moment Chelsea thought that maybe he hadn't heard her. But finally he said, "Your house?"

"Yeah," she said, smiling at him. "There's no one there. My mom's at work and my dad's in the hospital."

He kept his eyes on the windshield, but Chelsea could see a smile cross his face.

The smile made her feel warm all over.

He likes the idea, she thought.

He likes me.

I'm going to be alone in the house with a boy I like.

She felt excited and nervous and happy and worried all at the same time.

She closed her eyes for a few seconds, surrounding herself in silent darkness. When she opened them, she felt a little calmer.

She directed Will to her house on Fear Street.

He didn't make any comments or jokes about Fear Street, the way other Shadyside kids did when she told them where she lived. He probably doesn't know about this street, she thought. He's too new in town. He hasn't heard about any of the terrifying things that supposedly happened here.

Chelsea practically leapt out of the car. She *loved* Fear Street! It was the happiest street she had ever lived on. And this was the happiest night of her life!

He followed her up the walk. The front stoop was dark. She had forgotten to turn the porch light on.

She searched in her bag for the keys but dropped them on the top step. They both bent down to retrieve them.

He grabbed them first. She hoped he didn't notice how her hand was shaking as she struggled to unlock the door.

This is crazy, she thought. I have no reason to be this nervous.

She clicked on the hall light. She tossed her coat onto the front stairway. He removed something from his jacket pocket, then tossed his coat down beside hers. Then she led the way into the dark living room.

When she reached to turn on the lamp beside the couch, his hand gently took hers and pulled it away.

Before she had a chance to take a breath, he had wrapped his arms around her and was kissing her hard, kissing her until she could barely breathe.

"Will—" she whispered, pulling her face away, her heart pounding, her head spinning.

But he didn't let go of her.

He held her, tenderly but in a firm embrace, and guided her down beside him on the couch.

He kissed her again, long and hard.

She shivered.

She closed her eyes, then opened them wide. She wanted to see him, wanted to see everything. She wanted to see it all clearly, even in the dim yellow light filtering in from the hallway, wanted to see it so she'd remember it. Remember it for always and always.

She shivered again.

And realized she was cold. Still cold from their walk. Still cold from the drive back.

How can I be thinking about how I'm cold? she scolded herself.

How can I be thinking about anything at all?

He kissed her again, kissed her until they were both breathless.

The light from the hall seemed to shimmer. The whole room seemed to tilt and whirl, as if they were flying, flying on a magic carpet, high over the ground, looking down on the shifting, whirling, spinning darkness below.

Chelsea drew away, trying to catch her breath. As she closed her eyes and rested the back of her head comfortably against his shoulder, Will removed the length of cord from the back pocket of his jeans.

Silently he fingered it and prepared to strangle her.

chapter

13

Chelsea jumped to her feet.

Will let the cord drop to the couch.

"I'm so chilled," Chelsea said, wrapping her arms around herself, rubbing the sleeves of her sweater. "How about some hot chocolate?"

She was surprised by the disappointed expression on Will's face. His cheeks were two bright red circles. "Huh?"

"Hot chocolate," she repeated. "I'm going in the kitchen to make some. Okay?"

Why did he seem so distracted? Was it just his shyness?

Was he as excited as she was? After all, he had admitted that this was his first date too.

"Yeah. Great," he said, his expression brightening. "I'll help."

"No need," Chelsea said, starting across the dark room toward the lighted hallway. "But you can keep me company."

"Where's the bathroom?" he asked suddenly, standing up.

Chelsea pointed it out and hurried to the kitchen. She clicked on the light, filled the teakettle, and turned on the burner. She put two coffee mugs down on the counter. Then she walked over to the cabinet, reached up and pulled open the door, and searched for the envelopes of powdered hot chocolate mix.

This date is going so well, she thought happily.

She glanced at the copper kitchen clock above the cabinet. Eleven-forty. She wished it weren't so late. She wanted the night to go on and on.

She was still searching the cabinet, pushing aside slender boxes of spaghetti, when Will crept up behind her. He held the cord between his hands, leaving it slack enough to slip over her head. Once it was in place around her neck, he would pull it tight, as tight as he could, and wait for her to suffocate.

It wouldn't take long.

It was really quite easy.

Of course, it would have been easier if she had let him push her over the cliff.

He had been ready to push her up on River Ridge. One shove. So quick, so clean.

But she had decided not to cooperate.

Some things are worth doing the hard way, he decided, slipping silently behind Chelsea.

If something is worth doing, it's worth doing right.

He raised the cord, staring at her mousy brown hair.

His hand didn't shake, not even a tiny tremble.

That's because it's not *really* my first date, he thought.

He raised the cord higher. Up, up.

He was close enough to smell her lemony perfume, close enough to read the tag that was sticking up from the neck of her sweater.

He hated girls who didn't tuck their tags in.

His sister was a slob too.

Goodbye, Chelsea, he thought.

Good night.

He moved his arms forward, the cord in place.

The front doorbell rang.

"Oh!" Chelsea cried out.

He dropped his arms, struggled to change his expression, to make his face a blank.

"Will—I didn't hear you come in here!" Chelsea exclaimed breathlessly. She dropped two hot chocolate envelopes into his hand. "Here. Put these in the cups. I'll see who's at the door."

He watched her hurry out of the kitchen. Then, gritting his teeth angrily, he bent down and picked up the length of cord from the linoleum floor.

So close.

So close.

He glanced at the clock. Who could be there so late? Who could be interrupting their first—and last—date? Her mother? No. Her mother wouldn't ring the bell. Besides, Chelsea had said her mother was working all night.

Setting the hot chocolate packets down beside the two mugs, he crept to the doorway to listen, wrapping the cord carefully around his hand as he walked.

Wondering who it could be at this hour, Chelsea pulled open the front door. "Nina!"

"Oh, Chelsea," Nina wailed. "I just feel terrible coming here like this." Her eyes were red rimmed, her normally perfect straight blond hair completely disheveled.

"Nina, what's wrong?" Chelsea cried, holding the door for her.

Nina walked past her into the hallway, blinking under the bright hall light. "It's Doug. We had a big fight. I think he's breaking up with me, Chelsea. I really think he means it this time."

"Come in," Chelsea said distractedly. She looked toward the kitchen to see if Will was coming out.

It's so like Nina, Chelsea thought unhappily, to burst right in and not even ask if I have a date or if I'm busy or anything. She's so obsessed with Doug, she can't think of anyone else.

Nina caught her glance. "Oh, I'm sorry, Chelsea. Is someone here? You're not alone?" She followed Chelsea toward the kitchen.

"I have a date," Chelsea whispered, unable to keep a smile from bursting across her face.

"A date?" Nina whispered back, stopping to examine herself in the hall mirror on the wall. "With a boy?"

Chelsea flashed her friend a dirty look.

"I'm sorry," Nina said, raising her hands to her cheeks. I'm just so upset. I didn't know who to talk to. I've been crying and trying to drive and I thought—"

"Go sit down," Chelsea said, pointing to the living room. "I'll be right back. I want you to meet him."

Nina hesitated, then obeyed her friend's request. Chelsea hurried into the kitchen.

"Will, I'm really sorry," she said, keeping her voice low so Nina wouldn't hear. "I guess our secret date can't be a secret anymore. My friend Nina is here and—"

Chelsea stopped short. Her mouth dropped open.

To her astonishment, the kitchen door was wide open. And Will was gone.

chapter
14

"Can't you practice softly?" Mrs. Richards asked, peering over the news section of the Sunday paper. "I'm trying to read."

"Mother," Chelsea replied impatiently, "there's no way to practice a saxophone softly." She shuffled through the music sheets on the music stand she had set up in front of the couch.

"Maybe you could remove the mouthpiece," her mother said, her face disappearing behind the newspaper.

"Why are you always making jokes about my saxophone playing?" Chelsea asked, silently fingering the instrument, staring across the living room at her mother, who was seated at the dining room table, sections of the paper scattered out in front of her.

"I don't want you to get a swelled head," Mrs. Richards replied from behind the paper.

"Why don't you ever *encourage* me?" Chelsea asked, her voice rising several octaves.

"I don't *want* to encourage you," her mother said. "I *hate* the saxophone!"

Chelsea raised the instrument to her lips and deliberately made it honk as loud as she could.

Her mother jumped in her seat, nearly dropping the paper. She lowered the paper to glare at Chelsea. Then they both burst out laughing.

"Okay. Truce," Mrs. Richards said.

"Truce." Chelsea raised the instrument to her mouth and wet the reed, preparing to launch into her part in the Shadyside High Fight Song, when the phone rang.

Startled, she lowered the instrument to the floor and walked over to the phone. "Saved by the bell!" Mrs. Richards exclaimed gratefully.

"Hey, that was a short truce!" Chelsea exclaimed and picked up the receiver.

"Hi, Chelsea. Is this too early to call?"

It took her a moment to realize it was Will. "Hi. No. We've been up for hours."

"Who is it?" her mother called from the other end of the room.

"It's for me," Chelsea told her. She turned to the wall for a little privacy. "Hey, where'd you disappear to last night?" she demanded of Will.

"Huh?" Her question seemed to surprise him.

"Come on, Will," she said impatiently. "When I came back to the kitchen, you were gone. What happened?"

"What? Didn't you hear me yell good night?"

"No," Chelsea said.

"I called to you. I said I had to go. I thought I heard you answer me. Don't you remember? I said I'd call this morning?"

Chelsea didn't remember any of it. Was it possible that she just hadn't heard him? "Well . . ." She didn't know what to say.

She had been so hurt when she had found him gone. Hurt and confused. Finally she'd decided that he was feeling too shy to meet Nina. Or maybe he was so romantic, he really wanted to keep their secret date a secret.

"Well, I'm glad you called," she said finally.

"Who is it?" her mother called from behind her newspaper. "Is it a boy?"

"Mom—please!" Chelsea pleaded, holding her hand over the mouthpiece.

"Excuuuuuse me!" her mother cried sarcastically, loud enough so Chelsea missed what Will was saying.

"I'm sorry, Will," she said. "What did you say?"

"I asked if you wanted to go out tonight. You know, sort of finish our first date."

He's really sweet, Chelsea thought. She started to

say yes, but then remembered she couldn't. "I can't," she told him. "I have to visit my dad in the hospital, and I've got tons of homework. I haven't even started my writing assignment for Lash's class."

"Oh. Too bad." Will sounded very disappointed.

This had the opposite effect on Chelsea. Hearing the disappointment in his voice made her feel great.

"Uh—maybe you could come meet me after work tomorrow night," she suggested, surprising herself with her newfound boldness.

"Yeah. Okay," Will replied. "That sounds good."

She told him where the restaurant was and that it closed at seven. She warned him that she would smell of french fries when he picked her up. She always smelled like french fries after work. The grease smell seemed to stick to her hair.

"That's okay. I like french fries," Will replied.

They chatted awhile longer, about the movie they had seen the night before, about their short, chilly walk high above the river, about school. He seemed reluctant to get off the phone, which pleased Chelsea.

When she finally hung up and turned around, she was surprised to see that her mother had lowered the newspaper to the table and was staring at her from across the room.

"You've got a boyfriend?" Mrs. Richards asked.

"Mom, you don't have to sound so amazed!" Chelsea exclaimed angrily. "It *is* possible that a boy might like me, you know."

"I'm sorry," Mrs. Richards said quickly. "Is he the same boy you went on the date with? What's his name?"

"Yes. Will," Chelsea replied. "He's new in school too."

"That's great," her mother said sincerely. "When can I meet him?" Glancing at her watch, she tossed down the paper and stood up. "Oh, no. I've got to get going. I'm taking an extra shift this morning," she said before Chelsea could answer her question. A few minutes later she was out the door.

Listening to her mother drive off, Chelsea bent to pick up her saxophone. But her eye was caught by something out the window. It was snowing.

What a strange October, she thought.

Forgetting the saxophone, she stood up and took a few steps toward the big picture window that looked out on the front yard. An early snow with fluffy white flakes as big as feathers slowly drifted to earth from a windless sky.

How beautiful, Chelsea thought. It's so soft and pretty, it doesn't look real.

Deciding to get a better view, she ran to the front door and yanked it open.

"Oh!"

FIRST DATE

She gasped when she saw an enormous, hulking man in a dark trench coat on her stoop. His face was nearly pressed against the glass of the storm door, staring down at her with the coldest eyes she had ever seen.

chapter
15

Chelsea leapt back and started to slam the door shut.

The man's ice blue eyes narrowed. White flakes of snow clung to his short blond hair, to his bushy blond eyebrows, and to his massive shoulders. He raised one hand.

Chelsea hesitated.

What was in his hand? What was he showing her?

It was some sort of badge. A card above the badge said FBI.

The man took a step back and then another, as if demonstrating to her that he meant no harm.

Her heart still pounding, Chelsea hesitated, then pushed open the storm door a crack. The air was cold and wet from the falling snow. The sky was low and gray.

"What do you want?" she called out, more shrilly than she had intended.

"Sorry if I startled you," the man said in a thin, reedy voice, not the booming baritone Chelsea had expected from such a big man. "I'm Agent Martin of the FBI. Are your parents home?"

Through the snow, Chelsea could see a black Plymouth parked on the street, probably his car. Agent Martin continued to hold up his badge and ID card.

"No, they're not home," Chelsea said hesitantly, staring into his blue eyes. They were as clear as marbles. They stared back at her as if seeing right through her.

"Can I ask *you* a couple of questions?"

Chelsea nodded her head yes and pushed the door open wider. He lowered his badge, then shoved it into his trench-coat pocket. "I'll only keep you a second," he said, lowering his head as he stepped onto the Welcome mat. He followed Chelsea into the small hallway.

"What's your name?" he asked. Chelsea told him.

He wiped his well-polished black shoes carefully on the mat. Then he raised a big hand and brushed the wet snowflakes from his hair.

"Am I in trouble?" Chelsea asked, staring down at the small puddles forming around his shoes.

He smiled, a tight-lipped smile, but his blue eyes lit up, warmed for a second. He shook his head. "Nothing like that. My partner and I are canvassing the neighborhood," he told her. Then he quickly added, "You know—going house to house. We've been assigned to look for a young man."

"A young man?" Chelsea crossed her arms in front of her chest.

"We're hoping someone has seen him," Martin said. His eyes went beyond Chelsea to the kitchen. "You go to Shadyside High School?"

"Yes," Chelsea replied. "I just started last month. We're new in town."

"Nice town," Martin said dryly. Chelsea couldn't tell if he was being sarcastic or sincere. He turned his eyes to her. "Maybe you've seen the young man. He's medium height. Medium weight, only he looks like he works out. He's got well-developed arms and a good chest. He's got dark, curly hair. And dark eyes, almost black. When last seen, he was wearing blue jeans and a black leather jacket."

"I don't know," Chelsea replied. "A lot of guys look like that."

"Think about it," Martin said. "Anyone at school fit the description? Do you work? Maybe someone at work?"

With these words, a face flashed into Chelsea's mind.

Tim Sparks! Chelsea thought.

Oh, my goodness! Sparks fits the description perfectly!

"Is—is this boy dangerous or something?" she asked, unable to keep her voice from trembling.

Agent Martin nodded, his expression turning somber, his cold blue eyes narrowing to slits as he studied her reaction.

"Yeah, he's dangerous all right," he said. "And we have reason to believe he might be in the Shadyside area."

Chelsea started to say something but stopped. She couldn't decide what to do. Should she tell Martin about Sparks?

"If you've met anyone who fits this description, you should tell me about him," Martin said, as if reading Chelsea's mind. He shifted his weight, shoving his hands into his trench-coat pockets, staring at her expectantly.

"You said black curly hair?" Chelsea asked, stalling for time, thinking hard. "And looks like he works out?"

Agent Martin nodded.

Sparks always seemed so dangerous, Chelsea thought. I guess he really *is* dangerous.

"A boy came into my dad's restaurant where I work a few times," she said slowly. "I guess he kind of fits that description." She uncrossed her arms but couldn't figure out what to do with them, so she crossed them again. She leaned against the banister, feeling very nervous.

Martin pulled a small notepad and a ballpoint pen from his shirt pocket. He scribbled something on the pad.

Just like a TV detective, Chelsea thought.

"Did this boy give you a name?" Martin asked, keeping his eyes on the notepad.

"Yes. Sparks. Tim Sparks," Chelsea said. "He told me to call him Sparks. He said everyone called him that."

"Sparks," Martin repeated, writing it on the pad.

"He's been in trouble before?" Chelsea asked, picturing Sparks, thinking about how angry he could become.

Martin didn't answer. "Did you go out with him?"

"No!" Chelsea replied more loudly than she'd intended. "No," she repeated. "I just talked with him a couple of times. In the restaurant. He only came in a couple of times."

"Did he tell you where he's living, Chelsea?"

She shook her head. "I don't remember. No. I don't think so. He said he was looking for a job."

Martin wrote that information down, scribbling quickly, his eyes on Chelsea. "Does he go to your school?" he asked, lowering the notepad to his side.

"Huh?"

"Your school. Shadyside High. Have you ever

seen this boy Sparks in your school? Sometimes he enrolls himself in high school. He's twenty, but he looks about seventeen." Martin waited patiently for Chelsea's reply.

"No," she told him. "I've never seen him in school. Only in the coffee shop."

He asked her the name and address of the coffee shop. She told him.

"You've been very helpful," Martin said, shifting his weight again, shoving the pen and notepad back into his shirt pocket. He handed Chelsea a business card. "If you think of anything else that might be helpful, please call my partner or me. The number's on the card."

He turned and started to the door, leaving two dark puddles of water where he'd been standing. "If you see him again, call me—okay?"

"Okay," Chelsea replied, holding the card tightly in her hand.

"And don't take any chances," Martin warned. He glanced outside. The snow had stopped. There was not even a trace of it on the ground. His partner in a dark trench coat waited beside the Plymouth.

"Chances?" Chelsea asked.

"Play it safe for a while, okay?"

"Okay," Chelsea said softly, not moving from the banister.

"And don't lose my card," Martin said, pushing

open the storm door. "If you see this Sparks guy, call me right away."

He slammed the door hard behind him.

Chelsea watched him cut across the yard, taking long, bouncing strides, the big trench coat flapping behind him. Then she closed the front door, locked it, and leaned her back against it.

She closed her eyes, still gripping the agent's card in her hand.

Sparks had always seemed angry, but she had no idea he was dangerous. No idea he was wanted by the FBI.

And Sparks had actually asked her out on a date.

"Let's do something wild," he had suggested to her.

Something wild.

What would have happened if she had gone out with him? What would he have done to her?

And then she had another frightening thought: What if Sparks comes back to the restaurant?

What would she do then?

chapter

16

"*S*o where's this mystery boy?" Nina asked, scraping her chair against the floor as she pulled it up to the table. She pulled her lunch from the brown-paper sack. A vanilla yogurt and an apple.

"He wasn't in homeroom this morning," Chelsea said unhappily. Her lunch was spread out in front of her. A ham sandwich, a bag of potato chips, a container of chocolate pudding, and a Coke.

Nina must think I'm a total pig, she thought miserably. But if all I had for lunch was yogurt and an apple, I'd be starving all afternoon!

"Want some of this yogurt?" Nina asked. "I can never finish a whole container."

"No, thanks," Chelsea replied, taking a bite of her sandwich to keep herself from punching Nina.

Nina absently reached across the table and took a

handful of Chelsea's potato chips. "So tell me about Will," she said, her eyes on the double doors across the lunchroom.

"He's real shy," Chelsea told her. "And cute. His cheeks blush bright pink all the time."

"Cute," Nina repeated, not really paying attention.

"Who are you looking for?" Chelsea asked impatiently. She took a long drink from her can of Coke.

"Doug," Nina said, reaching for more of Chelsea's potato chips. "He and I made up last night."

"That's great," Chelsea said enthusiastically. "Maybe the four of us can do something this weekend."

"Uh-huh." Nina nodded without really hearing. "Hey—what happened to Will when I showed up at your house Saturday night? Why the disappearing act?"

Chelsea wasn't sure how to answer. She hesitated, then told Nina all about how it had been a first date for both of them, how Will had wanted to keep it a secret, their special night.

"Weird" was Nina's reply. Then she jumped up from her seat, having spotted Doug at the doorway, and ran to greet him.

Chelsea chewed on her sandwich, staring without focusing at Nina's uneaten yogurt and thinking about Will. She wondered why he wasn't in homeroom. Maybe he was sick. Maybe he wouldn't be able to meet her after work.

She was eager to see him, to talk to him. She was dying to tell him that she had talked to a real FBI agent. She was dying to tell him about Sparks, about how Sparks was dangerous and was wanted by the FBI, and how she had almost had her first date with Sparks instead of with him.

Will would like the story, she knew. He'd find it as interesting as she did.

She and Will were a lot alike.

That night the restaurant got crowded at dinnertime. Chelsea had trouble concentrating on her customers. She kept staring up at the neon clock, wondering if Will would show up at seven.

"Pick up!" Ernie called from the kitchen. He slammed his hand against the metal counter where he had set out the food plates. "Chelsea, you deaf or something?"

"Sorry." Chelsea hurried to pick up the plates.

"You're acting weird tonight," Ernie rasped, working a toothpick between his teeth. "You in love or something?"

Chelsea laughed. She could feel her face grow hot. She glanced back at the clock. Only six-thirty.

As she headed back to the counter, carrying an armload of dirty plates, someone tapped her on the shoulder.

Sparks!

Chelsea shrieked, and the plates fell out of her arms and clattered to the floor.

She spun around to see a middle-aged man with a shocked expression on his face. No Sparks.

"Oh, sorry, miss," he said apologetically. "I didn't mean to frighten you. I just wanted to ask for the ketchup."

Chelsea uttered a loud sigh of relief. "Sorry. I didn't mean to scream. I just—"

The man bent down with her and started to pick up pieces of the broken dishes.

"No," Chelsea insisted. "Please. I'll take care of it. Really. It's my job."

She finally persuaded him to return to his booth. Then she picked up the biggest pieces of china, swept up the rest, along with the spilled food, and dumped everything in the trash.

The half hour before closing seemed the longest half hour of her life. From his place behind the smoking grill in the kitchen, Ernie kept teasing her about being in love, cackling to himself, grinning at her and winking, which made the time seem even longer.

Calm down, Chelsea. Calm down. She repeated the words over and over, but they didn't seem to help.

By ten after seven the restaurant had cleared out.

Chelsea turned the lights down, almost to off, and emptied the cash register.

"Will, where are you?" she asked out loud, carrying the night's receipts to the small, one-drawer desk in the back.

Maybe he's sick, she thought. Maybe that's why he wasn't in school today.

She decided to call him as soon as she got home.

If he didn't show up at the restaurant.

She started to count the money, thought about Will, lost her place, had to start again.

The grill, she saw, hadn't been cleaned or turned off. It hissed softly in the background. The only other sound was the loud hum of the big refrigerator against the wall, and the steady *drip, drip, drip* of water from the faucet into the stainless-steel sink filled with dirty dishes.

Where's Ernie? Chelsea wondered.

He must be out back, all the way down the alley, emptying the trash.

Chelsea lost count again.

Okay, one more time, she told herself.

Then she heard the front door open.

The bell on the door jangled softly.

She tensed.

Normally she locked the door before emptying the cash register. But tonight she had left the door unlocked in case Will showed up.

The door closed quietly.

Footsteps out front. Coming closer.

Single footsteps. Just one person.

"Will?" she called in a tiny voice not loud enough to reach beyond the kitchen.

The footsteps stopped.

"Will?" she repeated, a little louder.

More footsteps, scraping against the soft tile floor.

"Will, is that you?"

Why didn't he answer her?

Suddenly frightened, she wadded up the stack of bills and shoved them into the desk drawer, quickly slamming the drawer shut.

She jumped to her feet, her heart thudding in her chest.

Where was Ernie? He was probably having a smoke by the Dumpster. Why was he always missing when she was in danger?

"Will, I'll be right out!" she called.

She bent her head and peered through the kitchen window into the darkened restaurant. She couldn't see anyone.

"Will?"

It had to be Will.

Please let it be Will.

chapter
17

Taking a deep breath she stepped out of the kitchen and behind the long counter. "Who's there?" she demanded, forcing her voice to stay steady. "Will?"

It was Sparks who stepped out of the shadows, one hand resting on the seat back of the first booth, a strange grin on his face.

Chelsea froze, gripping the edge of the counter. Why was he grinning at her like that?

His face was covered in shadow, but she could still see his gleaming, dark eyes and the evil leer on his face.

"Sparks—what do you want?" Chelsea cried, feeling her throat tighten in fear.

Stepping toward her, he looked so big. So dangerous.

He took a step nearer, then another. His dark

eyes, she saw, were watery. His normally pale face was flushed.

He giggled.

Is he trying to frighten me? she wondered.

If so, he's doing a good job of it.

She reached a hand under her apron into her jeans pocket and searched the pocket until she felt Agent Martin's card.

"Sparks? Are you okay?"

He giggled again, a high-pitched sound, almost an animal sound. He took an unsteady step toward the counter.

"Come here," he said, his eyes staring into hers but not quite focusing.

"Sparks—you've been drinking," Chelsea accused, backing up till she hit the wall.

"A few beers," he said with an awkward shrug. "Come here. Be friendly."

"No. Go away," she insisted. "I mean it, Sparks."

He shook his head. His expression became angry. "Hey, give me a break," he said, leaning against a counter stool. "I can tell you like me."

Staring at Sparks, wondering what he planned to do, Chelsea thought of Agent Martin's warning. She remembered the look on the FBI agent's face when she asked if Sparks was dangerous.

Yes, he's dangerous. Very dangerous.

What has he done? What crimes has he committed? They must be really horrible if the FBI is after him, she decided.

"Hey—come here," Sparks repeated more forcefully. As he leaned over the counter toward her, she could see that his forehead was covered with drops of perspiration.

"Sparks, please—" she started.

A grin spread across his face. He dived toward her, clumsily bumping into the counter.

"Ernie!" she screamed. But the fry cook wasn't there.

Gripped with panic, Chelsea turned and ran toward the kitchen. Just past the doorway she stopped and turned around.

Sparks was shaking his head as if confused, as if trying to clear his mind. "Hey—I'm just playing!" he called. "Just kidding around. Come here!"

Ignoring his plea and gripped with fear, Chelsea ran, sliding on the long, black rubber floor mat that ran the length of the kitchen. She headed toward the back door. Once out in the alley, she could run around to the front of the building and find help. It was still early, a little before seven-thirty, and the streets of the Old Village should have people on them.

"Hey, give me a break!" Sparks cried, stopping at the kitchen door, raising his powerful arms, pressing his hands against the doorframe, blocking the door. His eyes quickly surveyed the room.

"Go away! Leave me alone!" Chelsea screamed.

She grabbed the back door and pulled. It didn't move.

Her eyes went down to the heavy metal bolt. It was latched and locked. She was trapped.

"Hey, I won't hurt you," Sparks said, moving unsteadily toward her. "I'm just playing. Don't you want to play?"

"Sparks—please—go away!" Chelsea pleaded. She tore off the apron and tossed it to the floor. My only way out of here is to run right past him, she decided. He seems so unsteady, maybe it won't be too hard.

She took a deep breath and ran right at Sparks.

His eyes went wide. His grin grew wider. He reached out, intending to tackle her.

Chelsea dodged away from him, nearly banging into the still-sizzling grill.

Laughing loudly, he dived for her.

She made it past him.

Then she heard a *thud,* followed by a loud *hiss.*

She turned and saw that he had landed up against the steaming hot grill, his hand flat against the top surface.

He opened his mouth in a silent scream. Then finally the sound came, and he howled like a wild animal.

"My hand! My hand!" he shrieked and dropped to his knees in pain.

Chelsea stopped at the doorway.

"My hand! Oh—the grease! It's *killing* me!" Sparks howled. He rolled into a ball on the floor.

I've got to help him, Chelsea decided, hurrying back into the kitchen. I've got to help him—then call the FBI.

She got him to his feet and pushed him to the sink. "Here, Sparks," she said, turning on the faucet. "Cold water. Keep the hand in cold water. I'll call nine-one-one. I'll get an ambulance."

Uttering a low moan, his eyes shut tight from the pain, he obediently held the burned hand under the cold water. "Huh? Where are you going?" he managed to ask.

"To call an ambulance. I'll be right back."

Chelsea ran to the front, picked up the phone on the end of the counter, and reached for the card in her pocket.

I'll call Agent Martin first, she decided. Then I'll call 911.

Her hands trembling, Chelsea pushed in the numbers on the card. Pressing the receiver to her ear, she glanced back through the kitchen door.

Sparks was still at the sink, cradling his burned hand in his other hand, his face twisted in agony.

The phone rang once. Twice.

"Come on! Pick up!" Chelsea pleaded aloud, watching Sparks.

"Agent Forrest," a deep voice on the other end of the line said.

"Is—uh—Agent Martin there?" Chelsea whispered, cupping her hands over the mouthpiece so that Sparks couldn't hear.

"No, he's out" was the brusque reply. "Can I help you?"

"Yes. This is Chelsea Richards. At the All-Star Café. Please—"

Holding his hand, Sparks stepped up behind her.

"Oh!" Chelsea cried out, startled.

Had he heard?

"Did you reach them? Are they sending an ambulance?" he asked, his voice weak, his face twisted in pain, sweat pouring down his face.

"Sparks—go back and put cold water on your burn," Chelsea said, speaking into the phone so the FBI agent could hear Sparks's name. "I'm getting you an ambulance, Sparks."

There was a brief silence on the other end. Then Agent Forrest said, "We'll be right there. Keep him there. We'll bring an ambulance too. Are you in danger?"

"I don't think so," Chelsea replied uncertainly.

"We'll be right there."

The line went dead.

Sparks slumped into the nearest booth. He was moaning softly, resting the burned hand palm up on the table.

Chelsea clicked on all the lights. She stepped around the counter and stood over the booth.

"Are they coming?" he asked.

She nodded. "Let me see the hand."

She lowered her head to examine it. It was red and swollen. The skin had peeled in several places, and the open wounds were oozing. Pieces of skin were charred black where hot grease had clung.

After a few seconds Chelsea had to look away. She took a deep breath, forcing down a wave of nausea.

"Pretty bad," she managed to say.

To her surprise, he climbed to his feet. "It's not so bad," he muttered, avoiding her glance. "Maybe I'll go."

"No!" she cried, louder than she had intended.

He turned his eyes to her, his face filled with suspicion.

"The ambulance will be here any second," she told him. "You've got to get that treated. It's a really bad burn."

He stumbled toward the door. "No. It'll be okay. I'll go home and put a bandage on it."

"No—please," Chelsea pleaded.

She had to keep him there. She had to make him

125

stay until the FBI arrived. He was dangerous. Very dangerous. She couldn't let him go free.

"Here," she said, shoving a glass under the soda dispenser. "Drink this. Sparks, please. Sit down."

He hesitated, then turned back to her. She held up the glass of Coke. "Here."

"Hey, a free drink. This is my lucky night," he said bitterly.

Chelsea heard a siren outside.

Hurry. Please—hurry! she thought.

"Here, Sparks." She held the glass out to him.

"I've got to go," he said, raising his good arm and wiping the perspiration off his forehead with his jacket sleeve. "I'm kind of dizzy. Got to lie down."

"It's from shock," she said. "Sit down. Come on, Sparks."

The siren grew louder.

What's taking so long? she wondered. It seems like hours.

"Come on, Sparks. Drink this. It'll make you feel a little better."

He accepted the drink. "Hey, I was only kidding around," he said. "Just playing, you know?"

"I know," Chelsea said, eyes on the door.

Hurry! Hurry! she thought.

"I had a few beers, but—"

"Take it easy," she urged. "Drink the Coke. Please."

He had taken only a few sips when the front door burst open and two white-uniformed paramedics rolling a stretcher hurried into the room. "Where is he?" one of them, a tall, lanky young man with bright red hair, cried. He pointed to Sparks. "You?"

Sparks set the glass of Coke down carefully on the counter. He turned to the tall paramedic. "Burned my hand," he said quietly.

"Oooh—how'd you do that?" the other paramedic asked, staring at the hand, making a disgusted face.

"Just lucky," Sparks said dryly.

"Can you walk okay?" the tall paramedic asked. Sparks nodded.

"We'll take you to Shadyside General."

"Wait—" Chelsea started. Where was the FBI agent? She couldn't let them leave without him.

To her relief a man in a long, black overcoat appeared in the doorway. "Agent Forrest," he said, introducing himself loudly, holding up a badge and an ID card. His eyes went across the room to Chelsea. "You okay?"

Chelsea nodded. "Yes. I'm okay. But I'm glad you're here."

Sparks groaned in pain, then turned groggily to Chelsea. "What's going on?"

Agent Forrest pocketed his badge and stepped up

to the paramedics. "Take him to the hospital. I'll ride with him." Then he said to Sparks, "I'm Agent Forrest from the FBI. I just want to ask you a few questions."

"What's going on?" Sparks repeated, dazed and confused. He stared hard at Chelsea, trying to focus his eyes.

She looked away.

Forrest put a hand gingerly on Sparks's shoulder. "Let's get that hand looked at. Then we'll have a little talk."

"What have I done?" Sparks demanded. "What's this all about?"

He was still protesting as the two paramedics led him out the door, followed by the FBI agent. Agent Forrest disappeared, then poked his head back in. "You sure you're okay?"

Chelsea nodded.

"Want me to stay while you lock up?"

"No. I'm fine, really," Chelsea insisted. "I'll close up, then go straight home."

"We'll need to talk to you later," Forrest said, then disappeared again.

Chelsea exhaled loudly, slumping back against the wall.

Suddenly she heard footsteps scraping across the kitchen floor. "Who's there?" she cried, startled.

Ernie poked his head in from the kitchen window. "What's going on out there?" he asked. "Ready to close up?"

"Ernie—where were you?" Chelsea demanded.

He pointed toward the back door.

"Yeah. Let's get out of here," Chelsea said, sighing.

It didn't take long to close up. Ernie left, taking a bag of leftover fried chicken with him.

Chelsea watched him leave, then started to click off the lights. Her heart was still pounding, she realized. She felt trembly all over. Her fear lingered, even though Sparks had been captured.

"Oh!"

She cried out in surprise when she saw the dark figure standing in the doorway, outlined by the streetlight outside. In her fear it took her a few seconds to recognize him.

"Will!"

He gave her a shy smile and made his way toward her. "Sorry I'm late."

"Oh, Will—I'm so glad to see you!" Chelsea cried.

Without hesitating, she ran around the counter and into his arms.

The startled expression on his face quickly faded, and he hugged her back, holding her tightly. "I'm glad to see you too," he said.

Tonight is the night, he told himself, inhaling the

aroma of stale grease in her hair and feeling a little queasy.

He closed his eyes as he hugged her.

Tonight is the night, he thought.

Tonight is the night Chelsea dies.

chapter
18

As Will, sitting close to Chelsea on her couch, listened to her story, it was all he could do to keep from laughing.

He wanted to stand on the couch, raise his arms high in the air, and whoop for joy.

The stupid girl had turned the wrong guy over to the FBI. And now here she was, babbling on a mile a minute, telling him how frightened she was, how scary that poor clown had looked coming after her, how glad she was to see Will.

What a laugh, he thought.

She doesn't know what fear is—yet.

The house was empty except for them. Her mother was working all night, Chelsea had told him. Her father was still in the hospital.

It was perfect.

He couldn't ask for better, he decided.

It was too bad, really. He had actually liked this one. A little bit.

But there was no point in liking girls.

They only left you sooner or later. Like his mother.

They leave you and forget about you.

But I'll never forget, Will told himself.

I'll remember and remember and remember— until I find you, Mom.

And I'll find you. One of these days, I'll find you.

Chelsea was babbling on about her exciting night. She squeezed his hand.

With his free hand he reached into his back pocket. The cord. Yes, it was there.

Ready and waiting.

He had a sudden sobering thought. He narrowed his eyes, thinking hard, trying to shut out her voice so he could think.

The FBI. It wouldn't take them long to figure out that the loser that Chelsea had handed over to them was the wrong guy.

And then they'd be out on the prowl again.

They might even be after him. Following him. Following him no matter where he went.

He had always managed to keep a step ahead of them. This time they were close. So close. One of them had been right in this house.

Here he was wasting time, listening to this chattering girl.

"You look so concerned," Chelsea was saying. She squeezed his hand. "Come on, Will. Lighten up. I'm okay now, really."

That's another laugh, he thought, staring at her without seeing her. She thinks she's okay now.

Time to get this over with. Then get out of here.

She kissed him on the cheek. "It's so sweet of you to be so worried about me," she said.

"It's just that—you came so close," he managed to say with a straight face.

Enough fooling around, he told himself. It's time.

He suddenly felt cold all over.

The way he liked to feel.

"I have a confession to make, Will," she was saying. He realized she was staring at him expectantly, waiting for him to ask what her confession was.

"What?" he asked.

"I know I shouldn't have done this," Chelsea said shyly. "I mean, I know we talked about keeping our first date a secret and everything. But . . ." She took a deep breath. "I told my friend Nina all about you."

He forced himself not to react.

He didn't twitch, didn't frown, didn't move a muscle.

He had to think, had to think, had to think.

What now?

His first impulse was to slap her across the face

with all his might, to send her teeth flying across the room.

How could she have done this to him?

It was all so perfect. So perfect.

He had been in such a good mood. The FBI had the wrong guy, and he was about to show Chelsea her mistake.

She was staring at him, waiting for him to say something. He didn't move a muscle, held himself tightly in check.

I have to think first, he told himself. I have to decide what to do about this.

Then it came to him in a flash.

It was so simple, really. So clear.

There was no need to panic.

He'd just kill them both.

chapter
19

Will is so sweet, Chelsea thought. He got so quiet when I told him about what happened tonight. He was really scared for me.

He really cares about me, she decided. Which led her to confess about what she'd told Nina. And now, to her relief, he didn't seem to be angry at all.

His cheeks were bright red as always, but his eyes were warm, and he was holding her hand tightly.

"I'd like to meet your friend Nina," he said softly. "It's hard to meet kids at Shadyside, don't you think? It seems like everyone else has known each other since kindergarten. It's hard to break in."

"Yeah. I know the feeling," Chelsea agreed. "Nina is the only friend I've made so far. The other girls all seem so snobby."

Will let go of her hand and leaned forward on the

couch. "Do you want to ask Nina over? I'd like to meet her."

Chelsea smiled at him. "Sure." What a great idea, she thought. A chance to show Will off to Nina, to show Nina that she wasn't the only girl who could attract a boy.

She climbed to her feet. "I'll call her from the kitchen—if that's okay? Want a Coke or anything?"

"Yeah. Fine," he said, smiling back at her. "Tell her to hurry."

Chelsea made her way eagerly to the kitchen. She thought it a little strange that Will didn't want to be alone with her. But she was pleased that he was eager to meet her best friend. She had to admit that part of her loved the idea that for once she'd be the one with the boyfriend—not Nina!

Nina picked up after one ring. "Listen, can you come over?" Chelsea asked breathlessly. "There's someone I'd like you to meet."

"Is it that boy from your homeroom?" Nina asked.

"Yeah," Chelsea said. "He wants to meet you. And I've got an amazing story to tell you. You won't believe it. So will you come? Right now?"

"A hard invitation to turn down," Nina said, chuckling. "You sure you're okay, Chelsea? You sound weird. You don't sound like yourself."

"I'm just excited," Chelsea told her. "Hurry. Okay?"

"Be right there," Nina said and hung up.

Chelsea pulled a couple of cans of Coke from the refrigerator and started back to the living room when the phone rang. Setting the drinks down on the counter, she picked up the phone. "Hello?"

"Is this Chelsea Richards? This is FBI Agent Martin."

"Oh. Hi," Chelsea said. "I didn't expect to hear from—"

"Tim Sparks isn't the boy I'm looking for," Martin interrupted, speaking rapidly in a low monotone.

"Huh?" Chelsea nearly dropped the receiver.

"Wrong kid," Martin said flatly. "He's pretty close. He fits the description. But he isn't the right boy."

"Oh." Chelsea was speechless. Her breath caught in her throat.

"This kid Sparks will be in the hospital for a while," Martin continued. "The hand is pretty bad, and he seems to be in shock."

"I'm sorry," Chelsea said, her mind spinning.

She had pulled the phone cord into the hallway as far as it would go. Taking a glimpse into the living room, she saw Will pacing nervously, his dark eyes glowing excitedly, his black curly hair gleaming under the ceiling fixture. A short length of cord pulled taut between his powerful-looking hands.

Chelsea stopped short.

And realized.

"Oh, my God!" she whispered into the phone.

chapter
20

"Chelsea, what's the matter?" Martin asked, his voice remaining low and steady.

"I-I'm here alone with him!" Chelsea whispered, taking one last glimpse of Will pacing nervously with his length of cord. She backed silently into the kitchen.

"Huh? What are you saying?" Martin asked, losing his professional tone, alarm creeping into his voice.

"It's a boy I met in school," Chelsea whispered quickly, her eyes on the doorway, hoping Will wouldn't get suspicious and follow her into the kitchen. "He's here. In my house. A new boy. Will Blakely." She started to give a description.

"That sounds like him," Martin interrupted.

"Oh, no," Chelsea moaned. She suddenly felt

dizzy. She grabbed the kitchen counter, forced the room to stop spinning. "What do I do?"

"Get out of there immediately," Martin instructed. "Just put the phone down and leave the house. Get as far away as you can, Chelsea. We'll have men there in ten minutes."

"But—" She started to protest.

He cut her off. "Get out of the house—now."

The line went dead.

Chelsea replaced the phone with a trembling hand. The room was still spinning. The two cans of Coke seemed about to slide off the counter. Then the room tilted back up.

Chelsea crept to the hallway and listened. She could hear Will's footsteps as he paced back and forth.

What was he planning to do?

Why was he so dangerous?

Why had Martin sounded so alarmed?

She realized these questions were keeping her from making her escape.

Was she paralyzed? Couldn't she move?

Will seemed like such a nice guy, such a shy boy, so considerate, so caring.

He really seemed to care about her. He was the first boy ever to care about her.

That's what she had kidded herself into thinking.

That's what she was so eager to believe.

It was all a fantasy.

No. Worse. It was all a *lie*. A stupid lie.

She had been stupid.

So stupid she had hurt someone else—had hurt Sparks—because of a lie she wanted so desperately to believe.

Move, she told herself, still frozen in the dimly lit hallway, still listening to Will's steady footsteps in the other room.

Move. Move. Move!

And then all at once she was pulling open the kitchen door and hurtling herself out into the dark, cold night.

Onto the hard, frozen ground of her small backyard, the trees bending and shifting, black silhouettes against a blacker sky.

Where should I go?

What should I do?

And then she suddenly remembered Nina.

Nina was on her way over.

Nina would be there any second.

I've got to warn her, Chelsea thought. I can't let her come here. I can't.

Then she was running down the asphalt driveway, her sneakers pounding loudly, her arms churning at her sides, the cold air buffeting her face.

Running down the drive, running blindly through the darkness.

And then Chelsea stopped and cried out, a cry of horror as Will loomed up in front of her, his face hidden by the night, his powerful body blocking her path.

chapter
21

"Chelsea—where are you going?" Will demanded, his voice low and accusing.

She didn't answer. Panting loudly, her hands on her hips, she stared up into his shadowy face.

They stared at each other for a long moment.

Then she turned her eyes to the bottom of the driveway, trying to decide what to do next.

"Where are you going?" Will repeated. "Why are you out here?"

I'm not going to answer him, she decided.

I'm not going to make up a silly excuse. He wouldn't believe any excuse I gave.

She stared back at him in silent dread.

"Okay. Don't answer," he said with a shrug. "It doesn't matter. Let's go back inside and talk," Will said, moving closer. "Our date isn't over yet."

"No," she said, backing away. "I know who you are! Leave me alone!" Her voice was shrill and tight.

I'm going to run, she decided.

I'm going to run to the house next door. I'm going to pound on the door and scream for help.

Again, she looked past Will to the bottom of the driveway, hoping to see headlights, hoping to see FBI agents pull up, *praying* to see FBI agents pull up.

Fear Street was dark. The only sound was the whisper and creak of the bending trees.

"Don't run away, Chelsea," Will said softly, his voice nearly drowned out by the hiss of the night wind. "Let's go inside and talk about what's bothering you."

"No!" she screamed, all her fear bursting out of her in that one word.

She started to run.

He let out a cry, an angry cry, a wild cry like an attacking animal.

He caught up to her quickly and threw his arms around her waist in a running tackle.

"Oh! No!" she protested as she fell forward onto the cold, hard ground. Her forehead hit the dirt hard. Her head bounced back up, throbbing with pain.

He leapt on top of her quickly.

The cord slipped easily around her throat.

As he pulled it tight, she struggled to roll over. She turned to face him, her eyes wild with horror.

Good, he thought.

He didn't care if she watched him.

His muscles tightened as he tugged on the cord. She made a final choking sound.

Her arms flailed the air helplessly. She frantically twisted her body one way, then the other, trying to pull away from him.

But quickly she stopped struggling.

She's dead, he thought, checking to make sure she was no longer breathing.

That was easy. It took less than a minute.

So easy. Child's play.

Child's play. The phrase kept repeating in his mind as he rolled the cord around his hand, then jammed it into his pocket.

He stood up, filled with the usual feeling of excitement.

Of victory.

Of revenge.

He remembered he didn't have much time. He had to get ready for the next one.

Nina. That was her name.

He had to kill her too.

Then get away from the house—fast.

The FBI had never come this close to him before.

It meant he had to work fast. Real fast.

He'd kill the friend and be out of there in a flash.

This was odd, he realized. He usually didn't kill them until he got to know them.

He usually didn't kill them until after the first date.

But this was an emergency.

He really had no choice. No choice at all.

Next time he'd be more careful. Next time he'd find someone even lonelier than Chelsea.

His eyes on the driveway, he reached down and grabbed the dead girl's arms. Then he started to drag her to the side of the house, out of view.

Nina would be driving up soon. We wouldn't want Chelsea to spoil the party, he told himself.

He pulled her to the side of the house and left her behind some low shrubs. Breathing hard, he made sure the body couldn't be seen.

Child's play, he thought. Child's play.

He was standing in the driveway when he saw the headlights brighten the street. A car came into view.

He darted into the shadows as the car headed slowly up the drive. Then he made his way along the side of the house to hurry in through the kitchen door, which he found wide open.

One down, one to go, he thought cheerfully.

Most people wouldn't enjoy this, he realized.

But it was so easy. And so satisfying.

It made his hate melt away. All of the hate that weighed him down, all of the hate that he woke up with every morning and went to bed with every night, all the hate that kept him tossing and turning, wide awake when he wanted to sleep, all of the hate that drew him into the most frightening, painful dreams—all of the hate melted away when he killed one of them.

At least, for a little while.

He reached into his pocket, making sure he had the cord.

Then he straightened his sweatshirt and wiped the cold perspiration off his forehead with one hand.

He stepped into the living room just as someone knocked loudly on the front door.

chapter
_____

22

"Who's there?" he called, his hand on the brass doorknob.

"It's Nina," a girl's voice called in.

He pulled open the door and smiled at her. "Hi," he said.

She was short and pretty, perky looking with very short, straight white-blond hair.

Not his type. Not his type at all.

But he had to kill her anyway.

She smiled back. "Are you Will?"

He nodded shyly as she stepped past him into the hallway. "Where's Chelsea?" she asked, peering into the living room.

"Upstairs," he said. "She'll be down in a minute."

As he pushed the front door shut, he glanced

down to the street. No headlights. No cars. No one was around. Perfect.

He reached for the cord. He knew he had to work quickly.

Might as well strangle her there in the hallway. Why prolong it?

But Nina had already made her way into the living room. She tossed her blue jacket onto the floor, then dropped down into the big armchair across from the couch, tucking her legs beneath her.

She was wearing black leggings with an oversize T-shirt top. She shook her head to make her hair fall into place and smiled up at him as he entered the room.

"So you're in Chelsea's homeroom?" she asked.

"Yeah." He nodded.

He wanted to come up behind her, reach down over the chair back, and put the cord around her neck. But it was too late. She was staring at him. Watching his every move.

He hated it when they stared at him like that, as if he were some kind of specimen they were studying under a microscope.

"Chelsea's told me all about you," Nina said cheerily.

I know, he thought bitterly.

That's why I have to kill you.

"You too," he said shyly. "Uh—how long have you and Chelsea been friends?"

149

He was stalling now, thinking hard, trying to figure out how to get behind her.

"Not very long," she said. "Chelsea just moved here, remember?"

"Oh. Right. Me too," he said. He could feel his cheeks reddening.

"Do you work out?" she asked, staring at his arms.

"A little," he said.

"At a gym?"

"When I have the chance. I like it," he told her honestly. "I like to sweat. I like to push myself. You know. Push my body."

"I could tell you work out," she said, shifting her position in the chair. "You look really strong."

I *am* really strong, he thought. I'll show you how strong in just a minute.

His eyes went to the living-room window. He felt a stab of fear as the pale white beams of twin headlights appeared in the street.

Quickly he made his way to the window.

The car, an old station wagon, rattled past.

He breathed a sigh of relief.

"What's the matter?" Nina asked.

"Nothing," he said softly. "Thought I saw someone."

He realized he was behind her now. The chair faced away from the window.

Pulling out the cord, he stretched it taut between his hands and stepped forward silently.

She turned suddenly, twisting her head around to look at him.

He dropped the cord.

"Maybe I should go upstairs and see what's keeping Chelsea," Nina said, starting to climb out of the chair.

He quickly bent down and retrieved the cord.

"No. Really," he said. "She said she'd be down."

Nina got up and crossed over to the couch. She sat down on one end, facing him now. "That chair is so uncomfortable," she said, making a face. "It looks like it should be soft and comfy, but it isn't."

Will glanced out the window impatiently. Nothing but darkness.

Nina tapped her fingers on the arm of the couch. "Come sit down," she said, smiling at him. "You're making me nervous."

"Sorry," he replied. He obediently came around and sat down on the edge of the armchair.

"See what I mean about that chair?" she asked. "Sit back in it. You can't really tell how uncomfortable it is unless you sit back."

He obediently sat back.

I'm wasting time, he thought.

This girl is wasting my time.

I've got to finish. I've got to get out of here.

"Hey—Chelsea!" Nina shouted, cupping her hands over her mouth to form a megaphone. "Chelsea, what are you doing up there?"

Of course there was no reply.

Will pictured Chelsea's eyes goggling as he choked her to death. Once again, he saw her eyes roll up in her head, saw her whole body go slack, give up. He pictured her lying out there behind the low shrubs at the side of the house.

She was so easy, he thought.

Child's play. Child's play.

Why was this one being so difficult?

"Hey, Chelsea!" Nina called again, turning her head to the stairway beyond the living-room entrance. She turned to Will. "You sure she's okay?"

"Yeah. She's okay." He snapped his fingers. "Oh. I just remembered," he told Nina. "She went out."

"Huh?" Nina's face filled with suspicion.

"Yeah. She went out," Will said casually. "To get ice cream."

"Ice cream?" Nina's suspicious expression didn't change. "But it's freezing cold out. And Chelsea doesn't like ice cream," she insisted.

"She thought you might like some," Will said, feeling beads of cold perspiration break out on his forehead.

"That's weird," Nina said thoughtfully. "Where'd she go to get ice cream?"

"Out," Will said and uttered a high-pitched giggle.

Enough, he thought.

I'm wasting too much time.

I was hoping to get her without any screaming. But I'll have to put up with it. There's no one close enough to hear.

I really have no choice.

He stood up and pulled the cord between his hands.

"What's that?" Nina asked, recoiling on the couch, eyeing him with sudden fear.

He didn't reply.

Instead, he lunged at her, pressing her against the couch back.

She screamed and struggled, pushing at him with both fists, trying to knee him, trying to wriggle away.

But he was too strong for her.

Quickly he slipped the cord around her neck.

chapter
23

As Will tightened the cord around her neck, Nina raised her knees and kicked him hard in the chest. Will gasped in surprise and staggered back, struggling to breathe, his chest throbbing.

The cord. He had dropped the cord.

Nina screamed and scrambled off the couch.

He hated it when they screamed.

He hated it when they gave him such a hard time.

He'd have to teach her a lesson.

Desperate to get away, she stumbled over the low coffee table. Will grabbed up a heavy ceramic flower vase from the table. Swinging it in one hand, he turned to chase her.

She was in the center of the room, running awkwardly, her eyes wide with terror.

She screamed again.

Then, suddenly, she stopped and looked back at

him, breathing hard. "Why?" Nina asked, staring at the vase in his hand. "Why?"

"Sorry," he said.

He couldn't think of anything else to say.

How could he explain it to her?

Even if he could put it in words, he didn't have time.

"Where's Chelsea?" she asked, and then her mouth dropped open in horror. "You killed her? You killed Chelsea?"

He nodded. No point in lying to her.

"Chelsea!" she screamed. "Chelsea!" As if she didn't believe what he had told her.

He moved toward her quickly.

She had reached the hallway. She turned, her feet slipping on the bare wood floor, and headed toward the kitchen.

He couldn't let her go. He couldn't let her run out the back door.

He couldn't let her outside where she would scream for help, where someone might hear her.

Didn't she understand?

Didn't she understand that he had no choice?

"Chelsea!" she screamed. "Help! Oh, help! Somebody—help me!"

Her sneakers thudded down the short hallway.

He caught her as she reached the kitchen door-way.

He grabbed her shoulders from behind and

pushed her hard, and she stumbled forward into the Formica counter. The impact of the collision momentarily took her breath away.

He didn't give her time to recover.

She was up against the counter, gasping for air, trying to push away from it with both hands, as he swung the heavy vase and caught the back of her head.

She uttered a low howl and sank to her knees.

He moved quickly to finish her off.

chapter
24

As Will bent over to strangle Nina, someone grabbed his shoulders hard.

Someone pulled him back.

He stumbled, off-balance, startled.

Someone gave him a hard shove, and he landed against the wall.

Will recovered quickly and spun around to face his attacker.

"Chelsea!" he cried.

His dark eyes opened wide in terror and shock. Leaning back, he pressed both hands against the wall for support.

"Chelsea! No! I killed you!"

Standing in front of Nina, who lay unconscious, sprawled on the linoleum, Chelsea glared at Will. There were pieces of dead brown leaves in her tangled hair. Her jeans were stained with dark mud.

"I killed you! You're dead!" Will insisted, still pressed against the wall.

Breathing hard, Chelsea stared at him coldly, silently.

He raised an arm in front of his face as if to shield himself from her.

"No!" he screamed. "You're dead! You're dead!"

He stared at the dark red line that circled her neck, evidence that he had killed her, evidence that she was dead, dead like the others.

"I came back," Chelsea said breathily, glaring at him with menace.

His expression changed to anger.

Without warning, he lunged at her.

"You're dead! You're dead!" he screamed.

He tackled her around the waist. She felt solid. She was real.

Real. Not a ghost.

Dead. But real.

He pulled her to the floor, wrestling her down in front of Nina, who stirred but didn't open her eyes.

"You're dead! You're dead!"

With a loud cry Chelsea managed to pull free of him. He reached for her, but she was on her feet and stumbling to the sink.

He climbed to his feet—and stopped short.

Chelsea had pulled a large kitchen knife from the holder on the counter.

Her eyes wild with fury, her mouth open, she raised the knife high and ran at him.

As she reached him and brought the knife down, the gleaming blade aimed at his chest, Will backed up and kicked at her hand.

"Ow!" Chelsea screamed in pain.

Her hand felt as if it were on fire. The pain moved quickly up her arm and down her entire right side.

The knife flew out of her hand, bounced against the wall, dropped to the floor at Will's feet.

She grabbed her hand, tried to shake away the throbbing pain.

Will picked up the knife.

"This time I'm going to kill you for good," he said.

chapter
25

Gripping the knife tightly in his right hand, Will pushed himself away from the wall and advanced on Chelsea.

She faced him silently and made no move to get away.

"You can't kill me again, Will," she said calmly, almost teasingly. "I'm already dead, remember? You can't kill me again."

"No!" he cried. "It's not true!"

Then he realized she wasn't staring at him. She was staring beyond him.

He turned to the doorway to see two large men in black trench coats.

Both of them moved quickly toward him, their faces grim, purposeful.

What was gleaming in their hands?

Pistols. They both had pistols drawn.

"FBI," Agent Martin said, stepping in front of Will. "Drop the knife."

Will dropped the knife. "I killed her," he said, staring at Chelsea.

Martin, gun in one hand, clamped the other hand on Will's shoulder. Will sighed loudly and seemed to surrender.

The other one helped Nina to her feet. "You okay?"

Nina nodded groggily, rubbing the back of her head.

The FBI agent turned his eyes to Chelsea. "I'm okay too," she told him. "It was close, but I'm okay."

"I killed her," Will repeated to no one in particular. His eyes had become glassy, his expression uncertain. He looked pale and drained under the kitchen fluorescent light.

"I killed her."

"Quiet," Martin said with surprising gentleness as he clamped handcuffs onto Will. "You can tell us all about it later."

He turned to Chelsea. "What happened?" he asked. "Can you talk about it?"

"I guess," Chelsea replied, dropping down onto a kitchen stool. "He caught me outside. He must have heard me on the phone talking to you. He stopped me in the driveway and tried to choke me. With that." She pointed to the length of cord on the floor in the hallway.

"I *did* choke you," Will insisted. "I killed you. I know I did."

"I'm not as stupid as you think," Chelsea told Will angrily. "I pretended to die. I figured that was the only way to get you to stop choking me."

"But I checked," Will insisted. "You weren't breathing. I made sure."

"I play the saxophone," Chelsea told him. "It enlarges your lungs. I can hold my breath a long time. I can hold it for four minutes. I've tried it.

"I was so scared, so terrified," she continued. "But I pretended to be dead. I rolled my eyes up and slumped to the ground, and held my breath. It worked. He thought he killed me."

"And then?" Nina asked, coming over to put an arm around her friend's waist.

"I tried to get up. But I must have passed out. From being so afraid. When I came to, I heard you screaming. I hurried into the house. I knew I had to rescue you from him."

Nina hugged Chelsea tightly. "I'll never laugh at your saxophone playing again. I'll never tell you you should play flute instead. I promise," Nina said gratefully.

* * *

"I'm sorry," Chelsea said, sitting stiffly on the folding chair. She held her breath, trying to shut out the unpleasant odor of disinfectant.

"I'm sorry too," Sparks said. He was sitting up against the head of the bed, his entire arm wrapped in heavy gauze bandages.

They smiled at each other awkwardly.

"So I guess we're both sorry," Sparks said, chuckling.

A white-uniformed nurse entered briskly, checked the IV tube going into Sparks's arm, and left without saying a word.

"What's that for?" Chelsea asked, making a face.

"It's antibiotics, I think," he told her. "The burn got infected. That's why they're keeping me here. The IV doesn't hurt. It looks weird, but I don't even feel it."

"That's good," Chelsea said. She shifted her weight on the chair and turned her eyes to the window of the small room. "Listen, I really am sorry," she repeated, struggling to think of something to say.

Hospital visits were always so difficult. She'd been spending a lot of time in Shadyside General, visiting her dad. But she didn't seem to get any more comfortable during these visits.

"No, I'm sorry," Sparks insisted, scratching his dark hair with his good hand. "I'd had a few beers that night, and I never drink. Never. I don't know what made me do it. I guess I was just lonely."

He turned his eyes away, then continued, "I don't know what I thought I was doing there that night. I guess I was trying to be a big macho guy." He looked down at his bandaged hand. "I deserved what I got," he said softly. "I didn't mean to scare you like that—that night or any of the other times."

"But I had no reason to think that you were some kind of psycho killer," Chelsea said. "I just feel so guilty."

"Well, I was never entirely honest with you," Sparks confessed, turning his eyes to hers. "I ran away from home. My parents don't even know where I am. I just couldn't take their fighting anymore. So I came here to try to get along on my own. I'm going to go back to school. At night. As soon as I get a job and everything. But I've been really scared. I've never been so alone before. I guess that's why I was acting so weird."

"I guess we've both been acting pretty weird," Chelsea said.

He pushed himself up straighter, moving the flat, white pillows behind him. "Hey," he said, suddenly brightening, "maybe we should meet sometime *away* from that coffee shop of yours."

Chelsea hesitated. "You mean—a date?"

"Yeah." Sparks nodded. Then he added shyly, "If you think you want to."

Chelsea laughed out loud. "It's bound to be better than my *first* date!" she told him.

About the Author

R.L. Stine invented the teen horror genre with Fear Street, the bestselling teen horror series of all time. He also changed the face of children's publishing with the mega-successful Goosebumps series, which *Guinness World Records* cites as the Best-Selling Children's Book Series ever, and went on to become a worldwide multimedia phenomenon. The first two books in his new series Mostly Ghostly, *Who Let the Ghosts Out?* and *Have You Met My Ghoulfriend?*, are *New York Times* bestsellers. He's thrilled to be writing for teens again in the brand-new Fear Street Nights books.

R.L. Stine has received numerous awards of recognition, including several Nickelodeon Kids' Choice Awards and Disney Adventures Kids' Choice Awards, and he has been selected by kids as one of their favorite authors in the National Education Association Read Across America. He lives in New York City with his wife, Jane, and their dog, Nadine.

DEAR READERS,

WELCOME TO FEAR STREET—WHERE YOUR WORST NIGHTMARES LIVE! IT'S A TERRIFYING PLACE FOR SHADYSIDE HIGH STUDENTS—AND FOR YOU!

DID YOU KNOW THAT THE SUN NEVER SHINES ON THE OLD MANSIONS OF FEAR STREET? NO BIRDS CHIRP IN THE FEAR STREET WOODS. AND AT NIGHT, EERIE MOANS AND HOWLS RING THROUGH THE TANGLED TREES.

I'VE WRITTEN NEARLY A HUNDRED FEAR STREET NOVELS, AND I AM THRILLED THAT MILLIONS OF READERS HAVE ENJOYED ALL THE FRIGHTS AND CHILLS IN THE BOOKS. WHEREVER I GO, KIDS ASK ME WHEN I'M GOING TO WRITE A NEW FEAR STREET TRILOGY.

WELL, NOW I HAVE SOME EXCITING NEWS. I HAVE WRITTEN A BRAND-NEW FEAR STREET TRILOGY. THE THREE NEW BOOKS ARE CALLED FEAR STREET NIGHTS. THE SAGA OF SIMON AND ANGELICA FEAR AND THE UNSPEAKABLE EVIL THEY CAST OVER THE TEENAGERS OF SHADYSIDE WILL CONTINUE IN THESE NEW BOOKS. YES, SIMON AND ANGELICA FEAR ARE BACK TO BRING TERROR TO THE TEENS OF SHADYSIDE.

FEAR STREET NIGHTS IS AVAILABLE NOW. . . . DON'T MISS IT. I'M VERY EXCITED TO RETURN TO FEAR STREET—AND I HOPE YOU WILL BE THERE WITH ME FOR ALL THE GOOD, SCARY FUN!

RL Stine

Feel the Fear.

FEAR STREET® NIGHTS

A brand-new Fear Street trilogy by the master of horror

R.L. STINE

In Stores Now

Simon Pulse
Published by Simon & Schuster
FEAR STREET is a registered trademark of Parachute Press, Inc.

FEAR STREET® —

WHERE YOUR WORST NIGHTMARES LIVE

ALL-NIGHT PARTY

THE CONFESSION

FIRST DATE

KILLER'S KISS

THE PERFECT DATE

THE RICH GIRL

SECRET ADMIRER

THE STEPSISTER

By bestselling author

R.L. STINE

Simon Pulse
Published by Simon & Schuster
FEAR STREET is a registered trademark of Parachute Press, Inc.

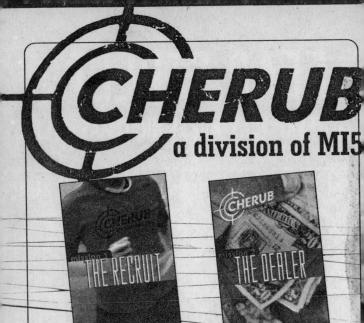